FAUX
A Novel

By Danielle Davenport

Dedication

To my son Drew: I thank God everyday that he saw fit to bless me with an amazing little boy like you. You may not know it, but you saved my life. You forced me to grow up and to be relentless in the pursuit of my dreams. Everything that I do, I do it for you. As long as there is breath in my body, know that mommy's got you. I love you!

Acknowledgements

First giving all of the honor and glory to God, who is the head of my life. I know that without you, none of this would be possible. You made 2017 rough enough for me to have no other alternative but to sit down and write and for that, I'm thankful.

To my mother, I love you so much. Thank you for being there when no one else was. Of course there is no way I can pay you back for everything you've done for me but I'm going to do my best to make sure you know you're appreciated.

To my family, thank you all so much for supporting every endeavor I've embarked on, celebrating my wins and forgetting the losses. I have the best grandmother, aunts, uncles, cousins and big brother that anyone could ask for. Granny, I have to reimburse you for so much gas money!

To my day ones Sabre and Jason, I love you all so much! Sabre we have been through everything a friendship could go through but you've stuck by me through every mood swing, every nervous breakdown, every crazy break up and every time I thought you would need to be on standby with the bail money. Jason, I'm so thankful for you. You keep me sane and I can always count on you to never leave me alone on the dance floor. Ya'll are coming with me everywhere.

To my day twos Gina and Candice, you all are the best friends I could ever have. You are more than my best friends, ya'll are my sisters and I'm so glad that I walked away from college with not only a degree, but two sisters that will be apart of my life forever.

To my Superman, thank you, thank you, THANK YOU. You've saved the day for me too many times to count and I'm so thankful that you are and always will be a part of my life. You're one of my biggest fans and you are always there to lift me up even when I don't believe in myself. Thank you for every word of encouragement and pep talk. I assure you that it wasn't in vain. I love you forever.

And last but certainly not least, thank you to everybody that has ever read a poem, a short story or a blog that I've written. You all have stuck with me every time I've deleted an entire website during one of my moments of self-doubt and you never stopped supporting. Thank you for every shared post, every like and every critique. I promise to make each and every one of you proud!

Chapter 1

I let out an exhausted groan and then rolled over to hit snooze one last time on my annoying alarm clock. I had been up late the night before tossing and turning due to the nerves about the meeting I had scheduled this morning with the governor of Indiana, Rich Pearson. Although it was two hours away, I had never had a meeting this big and I just wanted everything to go well. I took a moment to stretch before I finally pulled the covers back and stepped out of bed. Before I reached the bathroom, I took the time to switch on the Bluetooth speaker that I had on my vanity and put my R & B playlist on shuffle. As I waited for my shower to heat up, I took a look at the outfit that I had laid out the night before. I had spent almost an hour trying on suits and dresses before finally deciding on a navy blue pantsuit with a light pink shirt underneath. Deciding against changing the outfit again, I walked back into the bathroom and stepped into the shower. After washing up, I spent a few minutes just standing there and thinking about different things to say, best and worst case scenarios and anything else that could possibly go wrong. *Alright Fallon, chill out. You've worked hard for this. You're more than ready to make this happen*, I said to myself. After stepping out of the shower and drying off, I slathered myself down in body butter and began to get dressed. I decided on a sensible heel because I wasn't too sure how much walking I would have to do. As I was putting the finishing touches on my hair, the alarm from the intercom next to my front door began to buzz.

"Yes Archie?"

"Good morning Ms. Scott, I was calling to let you know that the car you requested is down here."

"Thank you so much. I'll be right down."

I put my shoes on and then pushed a button under my mattress that revealed a hidden compartment underneath the bed. I put the four-digit code in and a drawer slowly slid out. I grabbed my briefcase from the compartment and then pushed the mattress button again to lock everything back up. I grabbed my keys and my purse and then headed out of the door. As I made it down to the lobby of my apartment building my doorman, Archie, greeted me.

"Ms. Scott, Ms. Scott…you look beautiful as always. Why, if I were 30 years younger and didn't have the misses at home, I would…"

"You would what, Archie? You turn beet red every time I see you."

"You're right, you're right. I'm convinced my wife has a couple of screws loose because I don't know what would possess her to settle down with an old fool like me."

"Archie quit lying. You know you used to sweep the ladies off of their feet back in the day."

"Yeah well…I can't do too much sweeping these days. I just got this hip!"

Archie and I both erupted in laughter and then I told him to have a great day. I had been living in my apartment for over five years and Archie had been my doorman the entire time. He was such a sweet older man; he was about 6 feet tall and very stocky in build. You could tell that he used to be in the military but he honestly wouldn't hurt a fly. I walked out of the revolving doors to see that a Lincoln Town Car from the car service that I hired was waiting outside. The driver was standing next to the back passenger door smoking a cigarette but quickly flicked it away and opened the door once he noticed me walking towards him.

"Good morning Ms. Scott. Did you need to put any of your belongings in the trunk?"

"Good morning to you as well sir. No thank you, I just have my purse and this briefcase. I'll keep them in the backseat with me," I said as I gripped the handles of the briefcase even tighter. The driver waited until I was all the way in the car until he shut my door and then jogged around the back of the car back to the driver's side. As we maneuvered our way into the busy morning traffic, I pulled out my phone to answer emails and texts on the way to the governor's mansion. I opened my most recent text.

Hey Thing 1, good luck at the meeting today! I know you'll have no problem sealing the deal. 7:32 AM

—

9

I smiled while reading the text from my best friend and business partner, Taylor Smith. Taylor and I had been best friends since our freshman year of college and after graduating, we went into business together and started Smith & Scott Consulting. My parents died when I was a toddler and after bouncing around from relative to relative, after I graduated from high school, contact with my family was pretty nonexistent. Taylor had become the sister I never had. She was just as nervous about this meeting as I was but she had opted to stay at our downtown office instead of accompanying me to the meeting. Out of the both of us, I was the better talker and negotiator. Taylor was an expert with numbers. We balanced each other out perfectly. Just as I was about to reply to her text, the driver informed me that we were a couple of minutes away from the governor's mansion. I took a deep breath and tried to gather my thoughts and erase the nerves that were causing my palms to sweat. The driver pulled up to the gate and I rolled the window down and pushed the button on the intercom.

"Yes, how may I help you?"

"Fallon Scott for Governor Pearson."

"Can you please place your ID onto the scanner?"

I took my driver's license and placed it in front of what looked like a small television screen. A few seconds later, a faint green light could be seen scanning my ID. After a few more seconds there was a loud buzzing noise and the enormous iron gates in front of us began to open. The driver slowly crept forward and began driving up the narrow driveway that led us up to the house. When we got to the front there were two men who I assumed were security guards standing by the two columns in front of the door. They both had on black business suits and dark sunglasses covered their eyes. One of them came to my door and opened it.

"Good morning Ms. Scott, Governor Pearson has been expecting you. Sir…if you could please pull the car over by the fountain while you wait, I'd appreciate it."

The guard then helped me out of the car and then led me up the walkway to the front door. Once inside of the home I was asked to sit my things down and to put my arms up. The other security guard then took a magnetic wand and thoroughly scanned my body. He then directed his attention to my briefcase on the ground.

"Do you mind opening your briefcase and purse for me? I know you probably don't have anything to hide but its procedure."

"Sure. No problem."

I held my breath the entire time. Luckily, he didn't find anything and both guards led me back to the governors' office. As we walked down the hall I took in the décor of the home. There was a huge chandelier in the foyer and the entire home was paved with marble floors. As we walked by different rooms I could see housekeepers dusting, straightening furniture and cleaning the windows. As we made it outside of the governors' office door, one of the guards knocked three times and then waited for a moment and then knocked an additional four times. The door swung open and there stood Governor Pearson wearing a huge smile.

"Ms. Scott, it is truly a pleasure to meet you!"

"Likewise, Governor Pearson."

Rich Pearson was a jolly older man with salt and pepper hair and a dazzling white smile. Everything about him said 'politician'. He nodded towards both of the guards and they both pivoted on one foot and walked away leaving me alone with the governor.

"Please…come in and have a seat."

I walked towards the seat in front of the mahogany desk that was in the corner of the room and sat down.

"I'm very excited that you were interested in our services, Governor."

"Please call me Rich. We don't have to be so formal."

"Okay but only if you call me Fallon."

"Fallon…what a lovely name. I'm very excited about your services as well. I've heard a lot of good things and I said to myself, I have to bring them on board before I lose out on quality. Before we move forward, would you like anything to drink?"

"No thank you. I'm just fine."

Rich got up from the desk and walked over to the corner of the room where there was a tray full of assorted spirits. Pouring himself a glass of what I assumed to be straight Scotch, he walked back to his seat.

"So Fallon, how long have you been in the consulting business?"

"I've been consulting for about six years now. My partner and I decided to launch our company after college and so far, we've been extremely successful."

"So where would you say you see yourself and the company in say…5 years?"

"Honestly sir, in 5 years I would want to be settling down with a family and a dog or two in a house like this."

"Nonsense! You're great at what you do. I see bigger things in your future. And trust me, family is overrated."

We both shared a chuckle and it was then that I noticed his bare ring finger.

"I'm glad you've got a good sense of humor but it's time to get down to business. Your partner informed me that you all have drawn up some paperwork for me to look at discussing our pending partnership?"

"Yes sir we did," I said reaching down and grabbing my briefcase. "We have outlined our services for you for one calendar year, including where and how to send payment without it being traced back to this office. Please keep in mind that this is only a mock outline so the dates and prices can always be changed to accommodate your needs."

Rich took a few moments to read over the paperwork and I tried to read his expression but his poker face was remarkable. Once he got to the last page a smile slowly formed on his face.

"Everything looks great to me. You guys have really left no stone unturned. So do you guys offer the option of a free trial of services or am I asking for too much?"

"Yes sir we do. I was hoping you would ask that so I came fully prepared."

I stood up and put my briefcase on the desk. I then removed all of the contracts and folders that I had in there and placed them to the side. I carefully removed the lining at the bottom of the briefcase. I put on the pair of latex gloves that were in there and then carefully removed the kilo of cocaine that I had taped to the side of the briefcase. When I placed the white brick on the desk, Rich's eyes lit up like a kid at Christmas. He took a letter opener from the top drawer of the desk and slid the tip across the corner of the brick. He eased his pinky finger into the opening and dug out a little cocaine under his nail. He quickly snorted up the contents, then took his finger and rubbed it against his top and bottom gums. All of a sudden he just froze. I stared at him, half intrigued and half completely terrified.

"Rich is there something wrong?"

He looked at me and smiled. "No ma'am. Everything is right. Everything is right. Everything is right!" he yelled and then slammed his hand on the top of the desk, causing me to jump.

"As far as I'm concerned we have nothing further to discuss. Where do I sign, Fallon?"

Chapter 2

"Attention passengers, Nova Airlines flight 745 from Indianapolis to Miami is now boarding groups one and two at gate 3. Please have your boarding passes out and ready."

Taylor nudged me with her elbow and said, "That's us Thing 1. Lets go."

I snapped myself out of my daydream long enough to gather my carry on and headed to the gate to board our flight. After Governor Pearson signed on the dotted line for us to be his main supplier, Taylor and I decided to book a last minute celebratory trip to Miami. We had never signed a deal this big and this risky before but we were able to get the job done. We cleared our schedules for the rest of the week to enjoy a little fun in the sun. After placing my carry on into the overhead compartment, I took two steps to the right so that Taylor could slide into her window seat.

"You know what Thing 1? You can have the window seat. I'm going to put this neck pillow to good use and get some sleep."

"Are you sure? You love the window seat."

"Yeah, go ahead and take it. We wouldn't even be on this flight if it weren't for you."

Not one to argue, I slid into the seat and immediately put my seatbelt on. I put my ear buds in and pressed play on my R&B playlist. I didn't need to watch the safety video that they play before take off. I've seen those videos so much that I could tell you where the emergency exits and safety masks were off the top of my head. As we prepared for takeoff I looked over at Taylor, who had put her sunglasses on and wrapped her blanket over her shoulders. I smiled and turned my head towards the window and watched as we took off into the air and were immediately surrounded by clouds. It was such a surreal feeling. I couldn't help but take that moment to think about how all of this started and how the life that we live now almost didn't happen.

~~~

2006

"Excuse me, is this seat taken?"

I looked up from my plate of General Tso chicken and fried rice to see a tall, slender brown skinned girl with jumbo individual braids standing there and smiling at me.

I quickly scanned the crowded food court and smiled back. "No, no one is sitting there. Have a seat."

The girl placed her food tray down and sat down immediately.

"Thank you so much! You would think with us being in Texas we would be surrounded by southern hospitality but the people have been so rude here so far."

"You think so? The people have been pretty nice to me. Where are you from?"

"Baton Rouge, Louisiana. Where are you from?"

"I'm from Indianapolis, Indiana."

"Whew chile…you are a long way from home. What brings you all the way down here?"

"I'm here for school. I'm a freshman at TSU. What brings you here?"

"No way! For real? I'm a freshman at TSU too! Have you already moved into your dorm? I moved in yesterday and my parents left this morning. Which dorm are you staying in?"

"Well…" I hesitated. This girl seemed pretty nice but I wasn't exactly comfortable with telling her all of my business so soon.

She looked at me and tilted her head while she mocked me. "…Well what?"

I let out a small chuckle. It wouldn't hurt too much to let this girl in a little. Besides she was the only person I had met after two days of being in Houston and honestly, I needed a friend.

"Well when I went to get my room assignment they told me that there weren't anymore rooms available so I would have to wait until they called me when they had an opening."

The tall stranger furrowed her brow and I could see her jaw clench.

"Girl that is a lie! I know for a fact that the girl that was supposed to be my roommate isn't coming. We went to high school together and

---

15

she was supposed to room with me but she got pregnant and stayed in Baton Rouge. We're about to go to this registrar's office and cause a scene! Where have you been staying?"

"Well…" I hesitated again. "Last night I slept in my car and…"

"GIRL. NO." The tall stranger all but screamed at me. "Get your stuff and let's go. Here, bring this with you", she said as she grabbed my Styrofoam food container and picked up her food too.

"By the way, my name is Taylor. Taylor Smith."

"Nice to meet you Taylor. I'm Fallon Scott."

We headed to my car in the Galleria Mall parking lot and headed back to campus. I had initially come to the mall to look for a job just in case I had to rent a room somewhere. I had come down to Houston all by myself. My family and I weren't close at all. After my parents died they made it known every chance they got that they couldn't wait for me to graduate from high school so that they wouldn't have to be responsible for me anymore. I had spent the summer bouncing from couch to couch at all of my friends' houses. I had a little money saved from the two summer jobs that I had gotten just to pass the time and have a little cash to support myself. Once it was time for me to begin my first semester of college, I packed my car up with as much of my belongings as it could handle and made a vow to never look back. What are the odds of me randomly meeting someone as soon as I got here and ending up with a potential roommate? I'm glad I let her sit down.

When we got to campus Taylor and I marched into the registrars' office and like she promised, Taylor caused a huge scene. She yelled and screamed and threatened to sue the school. Just to shut her up and get her out of their hair, they finally gave me the keys to our room. We drove over to our dorm and began unloading all of my stuff and bringing it into our room. After a couple of trips, a group of guys that were standing in front of our dorm offered to help. At that point Taylor and I were exhausted so we happily obliged. We sat on the hood of my car and got a good look at our moving helpers.

"Are all the men down here this fine?"

"Yes they are but I would steer clear of this particular bunch. This is just community service for them," Taylor said as she rolled her eyes. It was at that moment that I finally paid attention to the camouflage shorts and spray painted gold boots that they had on. Once they loaded the last few plastic totes from my trunk into our room, one of the more attractive helpers came up to me and handed me a flyer. He was tall, had smooth light brown skin and had long braids that were braided in all kinds of designs and hung past his shoulders. He opened his mouth and the sun hit his braces as he began to speak to us.

"I'm not exactly sure if you ladies already had plans tonight but we're having a Back to School party and we would love it if you all could come."

This would be my first college party. I was a little nervous. "Will there be food there?"

The gorgeous moving helper laughed and showed me all 32 of his pearly whites. "Yes, there will be all the barbecued chicken and Omega Oil your little pretty self can handle."

"Omega Oil? What's Omega Oil?"

"Girl, a death trap", Taylor said. "But thank you. We'll be there."

The guy smiled and said, "Alright now, I'll be looking for you. Since I helped you move in you owe me a dance." He winked at me and then turned and walked away with his purple clad crew. I watched him walk away for a while but the sound of Taylor talking interrupted my thoughts.

"Girl it's the first party of the year so you know it's going to be too live! Lets get your stuff unpacked so we can start getting ready."

We went back to our room. I unpacked and got my side of the room together while Taylor sat on the edge of her bed and broke down the contents inside of a small plastic bag.

"Fallon do you smoke?"

"Every now and then. Don't we have to go outside?"

Taylor giggled while she filled and licked a cigar wrapper to seal it. "Girl, as much as we pay for this room we can do whatever we want in here."

She hopped off of the bed and walked over to her side of the closet and took out a towel. She rolled the towel up and placed it at the bottom of the door. She then walked back over to her dresser and lit a strawberry scented candle that she had sitting on top of it.

"Alright, we should be good to go now."

We spent the next few hours pre-gaming, getting to know one another, trying on different outfits, and I did my hair. I had recently gotten it cut into a short pixie cut so it didn't take that long. Around 11 o'clock we decided to head out to the party. The party wasn't too far from campus, which was a good thing because I was still trying to learn my way around Houston. When we pulled up to the venue

---

the entire parking lot was packed with students and Houston locals. The party venue was located in a strip mall so we had to drive around the huge parking lot a few times to even find a spot. We finally found a spot not too far from the front door. Before we walked in we replaced our flip-flops with the heels we had carried with us. Once we got to the door two bouncers, a man and a woman greeted us. Another girl was standing there talking to them. She wasn't security but she looked too sophisticated to be a student either. She stood there in silence as the man checked our ID's and placed big black x's on our left hands. The woman came over and scanned our bodies with a magnetic wand and then did another check by patting down our legs, arms, and making sure we hadn't hid anything in our bras. You can never be too safe I guess. "Alright ladies, you guys are good to go. You made it here before midnight so it's free to get in. You ladies have a great night." We thanked the security guards and opened the doors to the venue. The music was so loud that it felt like the bass was vibrating through our bodies. Once inside we stopped to scan the room and take in the scene. The dance floor was packed with people. The DJ was located on a raised platform towards the back of the room. To my left there was a makeshift bar that was full of orange coolers and plastic red cups and napkins. To my right there were rows of chairs that were all occupied by girls whose shoes had already checked out on them. The scene was a bit chaotic and I'll admit, I was a bit overwhelmed. Taylor snapped me out my daze by grabbing my arm and saying, "Come on girl, let's dance! This is my song!" We made a beeline towards the middle of the floor and I began to sway my hips back and forth as Young Dro-Shoulder Lean blasted through the speakers. Two seconds after I started dancing, I felt a pair of hands slide around my waist and the stranger behind me began to match my movements and dance with me. I looked at Taylor and mouthed, "Is he cute?" Taylor smiled and gave me the thumbs up signal so I continued to grind my hips on him. As soon as I began to break a sweat, the DJ scratched the record a few times and then the song switched to George Clinton-Atomic Dog. The crowd erupted into a collective "Ohhh!" and the dance floor parted to make way for a group of guys that were hopping around and barking. I noticed a few of them were the ones that helped us that morning but I didn't see the fine one that had invited us to the party. Some of them were dressed in their purple shirts and camouflage shorts, others were

---

18

shirtless and there were a couple that was completely naked with Crown Royal bags taped to their crotches. They hopped around for what seemed like the entire song and as the line moved around the room, I finally caught a glimpse of the handsome helper from before. He wasn't hopping, but he was walking alongside the line with his hooks in the air. As the front of the line rounded the corner to hop back to the back of the room, the handsome helper finally glanced my way and immediately started smiling. He made his way over to me and grabbed my hand.

"I was hoping you would make it, beautiful. Can I get you something to drink?"

"Sure."

He led me towards the makeshift bar and one of his fraternity brothers fixed us two plastic cups of Omega Oil. I took a sip and immediately wished that I hadn't. Taylor was right; it was terrible. I didn't want to be rude though so I suffered through it.

"Are you having a good time tonight?"

"Yes I am. What about you?"

"I am. Can't you tell?" We both laughed as he wiped the sweat dripping from his neck and his braids.

"So if you don't mind me asking, what's your name?"

"My name is Smoke. What's yours?"

I smacked my lips. "No, what did your mother name you? I know she didn't name you Smoke."

He laughed. "My name is Xavier. Everybody calls me Smoke though."

"It's nice to meet you Xavier. My name is Fallon."

"Fallon…beautiful name for a beautiful girl."

"Thank you. You know, I never did get to thank you all for helping me move in today. I really appreciate the help."

"No problem. We wouldn't just let you move all of that stuff in by yourself. It may be too soon for me to ask you this but…would you mind if I got your phone number? I'd love to get to know you more without all of this craziness going on."

"I don't know…you're not trying to get me drunk on this Omega Oil and take advantage of me, are you?"

Xavier laughed again. "I promise you, I'm the perfect gentleman. After I helped you move earlier I talked about you for the rest of the day. I was pissed that I hadn't asked you for your name and number then."

"Yeah right. I don't believe you."

"You don't believe me? I can prove it to you. Hey Mike! Mike!" He yelled to get the attention of his fraternity brother that was fixing the drinks. Mike handed a plastic cup over to a girl that had been waiting in line and walked over to us.

"What's good bro?"

"Can you please tell my new friend Fallon here that I was talking about her for the rest of the day after we left the dorms?"

Mike chuckled. "He did. He was saying how he hoped you were coming to the party because he forgot to ask you for your name."

I looked back at Xavier and he was staring at me, smirking. "See, I told you I wasn't lying."

"I guess you did. Well thank you Mike for that confirmation."

"No problem. Aye, but what's good with your friend that you were with earlier though?"

"She's out there on the dance floor. You should go and dance with her."

Mike threw the dishtowel that he had in his hands up on the counter and said, "Bet. You don't have to tell me twice." He ran off and disappeared into the crowd.

Xavier and I both laughed. "So now that you see that I'm a good guy, can I have your phone number?"

"Sure, but only if I can have yours as well."

We swapped cell phones and I put my number in his as he put his number in mine. As I was handing him his phone back one of his other fraternity brothers came up to him.

"Aye Smoke, we need you at the door bro."

"Okay, here I come," he said and then turned back to me. "I'll be right back so don't disappear. You still owe me a dance."

"Okay I won't."

I stood there for a few moments sipping my drink and watched as Xavier and his frat brothers huddled around the door. After a minute or two I decided that he would just have to come and find me. I walked back to the dance floor to find Taylor. I found her dancing on the bartender, Mike. As soon as I got her attention, she stopped dancing and walked over to me.

"Girl I've been looking for you! Are you having a good time?"

"Yeah I'm having a ball. I can see that you're having a good time."

"Girl this party is everything! Walk to the bathroom with me."

We maneuvered through the sea of people and made our way to the bathrooms at the back of the venue. Once we got inside, Taylor talked to me from one of the stalls while I fixed my makeup and hair in the mirror. There was one other girl in the bathroom with us. I glanced in the mirror and noticed it was the girl that had been talking to security when we first got there. She was fixing her makeup too. "Thanks for telling Mike to come and find me. He is fine as hell! Did you get the dudes number that helped us earlier? I saw you walk off with him."

"Yeah, we exchanged numbers. He seems really cool. This party is live though!"

The girl standing next to me at the mirror giggled. "This party isn't that great. Let me guess…you guys are freshman?"

I nodded my head yes.

"Well if you guys are interested in a real party I can take you to one. It's a club downtown that I can get you into."

"But we're only 18."

"Don't worry about all of that. I can get you in. Trust me. My name is Draya, by the way."

"Nice to meet you Draya. I'm Fallon, and that's my roommate, Taylor."

Taylor walked out of the stall and came over to the sink to wash her hands. She dried them off and then extended her hand to Draya.

"Nice to meet you. I'm definitely down to go to the club. Do you want to ride with us or what?"

"No, I drove. You guys can follow me downtown."

"Okay cool."

We left the bathroom and made our way to the door. I turned around and scanned the crowd to see if I could see Xavier anywhere but he was nowhere to be found. I guess that dance would have to wait.

We all got into our cars and we followed Draya out of the parking lot, away from the strip mall and onto the freeway. Around 15 minutes later we pulled up at a club named Life. It was an eerie gray color and it reminded me of a house that you would see in New Orleans. After circling the block a few times to find a parking spot, we finally found one not too far away from the club. As we were walking up to the door I could see Draya standing on the corner waiting for us. Draya was tall and slender and had legs that went on for what seemed like forever. Her naturally sandy brown hair was cut into a cute bob and she had green eyes that seemed to pierce right through you. She was only standing there waiting on us but you would've thought she was in the middle of a photo shoot. When she finally spotted us she smiled and said, "Come on guys. Make sure you let me do all the talking."

We were too nervous to do much talking anyway. We walked past the crowded line at the front and went to a side door. Draya banged on the door as hard as she could and it immediately swung open. An enormous bald man stood there snarling at us until he seen Draya standing there. He immediately softened up.

"Draya Baby. I was hoping I would see you tonight. Who are your friends?"

"Hey Tone" she said and reached for a hug. "These are my friends Taylor and Fallon."

"Are these good girl friends or bad girl friends?"

"Now Tone, you know I only hang with good girls."

"Yeah okay. That's what you said last time. Do you want your usual table?"

"Please. And bring a couple of bottles for me and my friends, if you don't mind."

Tone cleared the doorway and motioned for us to come in. As we walked past him I could hear him saying, "Mmm, mmm, mmm," under his breath. I was immediately uncomfortable. Tone led us to what appeared to be the VIP area and pulled out our chairs for us. Draya could sense that were tense.

"Come on ya'll, loosen up! Make it look like you belong in here."

We tried to relax. Both of us stood up and started dancing with one another. A few minutes later two bottle girls walked up to us with sparklers and big bottles of champagne. They also handed us a tray full of shots. "Those are courtesy of Eric Moulds and his friends over there," the girl said as she pointed over to another VIP area full of men that just so happened to be staring and smiling our way. We all raised the shots their way as a way of saying thank you and proceeded to down them. My chest began to burn immediately. Draya poured herself a glass of champagne and then leaned over and began to yell over the music.

"So how are you ladies liking Houston so far?"

"It's okay. Its only our first week here so we haven't really gotten out and explored that much."

"There's plenty of time for that. Let me ask you something though. Are you ladies interested in making a little money while you're here for school?"

Taylor and I looked at each other and then looked back at Draya. "I'm always looking to make some money. What would we have to do?" Taylor asked.

Draya smiled and flipped her hair out of her face. "Nothing that you wouldn't want to do. Trust me, its legit and easy money. I'll talk to you all more about it later when I can talk without screaming." Just then another waitress came over with another tray of shots. "Hey ladies, these are courtesy of Rafer Alston and his crew over there." We waved and thanked them for the shots and quickly threw them back. As the shot began to take effect in my system, I stood up and began dancing all by myself and looking down at the crowd. The club was packed with people and the VIP area was full of athletes and rappers. The DJ was really good and did a great job of mixing all of the popular songs with the old chopped and screwed classics. I was in the zone and having a great time. At least I was…until I turned around and seen Taylor leaning over the table and snorting white lines off of the tabletop.

"Taylor! What are you doing?"

Draya laughed. "Calm down Fallon. She's just having a little fun. I thought you said you wanted to have a real party."

"I don't have to do THAT to have a good time."

"It's cool Fallon. You don't have to do anything you don't want to do. Just relax and enjoy yourself."

At that point I was more than ready to go. I wasn't sure who Draya was or what she had going on but I wanted nothing to do with it. I couldn't believe Taylor either. Smoking a blunt in our dorm room was one thing, but cocaine? I wanted no parts of any of that. I tried to shake off my disdain for what I just witnessed and poured myself another glass of champagne. I went back to dancing and admiring the crowd. I noticed Tone making his way towards the VIP area with a nervous look on his face. My eyes followed him as he made his way up the steps and directly over to our table to Draya. He grabbed her arm and whispered something in her ear. Whatever he said made all of the color drain from her face and she quickly gathered her things and came up to me and said, "I'll be right back. Keep an eye on you friend."

Tone and Draya walked down the steps to a back hallway behind the bar of the club and near the bathrooms. I wasn't sure what was going on but it definitely had Draya shook. I continued to dance but moved away from the balcony and opted to stand right next to Taylor, who definitely didn't need any more drinks or anything else for the rest of the night. She was barely functioning. The DJ got on the mic and informed us that it was last call for alcohol. I knew that last call meant that the club was going to close and I didn't want to just leave without telling Draya goodbye. She hadn't been gone that long so I decided to go look for her. I told Taylor I would be right back. I didn't want to leave her by herself but it wasn't going to take me that long to say good-bye and come right back. I walked down the steps of the VIP area and made my way towards that dark hallway where I last seen Tone and Draya. There were only two doors on either side of the hallway so I cracked open the door to my right. It was nothing but a storage closet with cleaning supplies in it. I slowly cracked the door to my left and could see Draya sitting down in a chair with tears streaming down her face. A short dark skinned man with a head full of beautiful curly hair was standing in front of her. He was dressed in a black dress shirt and black dress slacks with a sharp crease in them. He had no other jewelry on except for a large gold watch that looked fairly expensive from where I was standing. I was really confused by Draya's tears until he began to speak.

"I specifically asked to you to bring me people that are dependable and are ready to work and you bring me two young girls…again!"

"I'm sorry Goldie. I couldn't find anybody else. We don't have to use them if you don't want to but please don't hurt them."

"Oh I'm not going to lay a finger on them. I'm leaving that up to you." He reached behind his back and pulled out a small silver pistol. As he handed it over to Draya she softly pushed his hand away and sobbed even harder.

"No Goldie. Please. I can't do this again. Please don't make me-"

Goldie interrupted her by reaching back and slapping her so hard that saliva flew from her mouth. I covered my own mouth to stifle a gasp that was desperately trying to come out.

"Don't you ever put your hands on me! Do you understand me?" He stepped forward and snatched a handful of Draya's hair and raised her out of the chair and directly into his face.

"You brought those young bitches into MY club and had them snorting cocaine off of the table top. How stupid could you be?

———

They've seen way too much and they know way too much. Now you're going to get rid of them tonight or I'm going to have Tone get rid of you."

He released her hair and shoved her back into the chair. He handed the gun over to her and this time she reluctantly took it.

At that moment I heard the familiar sound of the AT&T ringtone from a Motorola Razor. I stood there staring at Draya and Goldie to see if either of them would get their phone that was ringing but they both looked towards the door at me. It was at that moment that I realized that it was my phone that was ringing. I pulled it out and rushed to try and turn the ringer off but it was too late. I looked at the screen. It was Xavier.

"Looks like we have company, Draya. Won't you please join us?" Goldie walked towards the door and extended his hand to me. I slowly put my hand into his and he escorted me to the chair next to Draya. My entire body was shaking.

"What's your name sweetheart?"

"My name is F-F-Fallon." I managed to stammer out.

"No need to be nervous my dear. I'm not going to hurt you. I do have a few questions for you though and I want you to be completely honest with me. You seem like a good girl and I like to make new friends. Would you like to be my friend Fallon?"

I could barely speak. "I'd love to be your friend, sir."

"Good. And please, just call me Goldie. Now the only thing that would make us enemies is if you lie to me and you wouldn't do that to me, now would you Fallon?" I shook my head no.

"Good, good, good. So Fallon, I need you to tell me everything that you heard here tonight. And don't leave anything out."

My mind was going a mile a minute. I didn't want to lie but telling the truth would get me and Taylor killed. "I didn't hear anything sir. I had just walked up to look for Draya when my phone rang."

Goldie began to laugh. "Fallon I thought you wanted to be my friend? My instructions were clear; all you had to do was tell the truth. You've left me with no other options." He grabbed the gun from Draya's hands and began screwing on a silencer barrel that had been sitting on his desk.

"Okay, wait a minute Goldie. I will tell you everything just please don't hurt me or my roommate."

—

25

Goldie stood there staring at me for a few seconds before he leaned back on the desk and crossed his arms in front of him, the gun still in his hand. "I'm listening."

"I came to look for Draya to let her know that we were leaving and I found you both sitting in here talking. I came in when I heard you saying that you were looking for dependable people to work with and not two young girls like before. I'm not exactly sure what you're looking for sir, but I'm here to tell you that you're about to make a huge mistake by not wanting to work with us."

Goldie squinted and a small smirk appeared on his face. "I'm making a mistake, huh? How so?"

"Well my roommate and I may be young, but we're both book and street smart and self-sufficient. I'm a Computer Science major and Taylor is an Accounting major. Even though we're both only freshman, I think that that could be very beneficial to you and your business. What better way to infiltrate a college campus than to have students that actually go there to be your eyes and ears?"

Goldie sat there for what seemed like an eternity just staring at me and twirling the hairs of his goatee in between his fingers. No one said a word; the only noise that I could hear was the sound of my heart thumping through my chest. Goldie finally laid the gun down on the desk and I let out a sigh of relief.

"Okay Ms. Fallon. Let's do business."

Chapter 3

"Ladies and gentlemen, welcome to Miami International Airport. Local time is 1:37 PM and the temperature is a balmy 85 degrees…" I snapped myself out of my daze to see that we had landed in Miami. I unhooked my seatbelt and used the little room that I did have to stretch. I looked over at Taylor who was sleeping so hard that her mouth was open. I gently shook her.

"Wake up Thing 2. We're in Miami."

Taylor looked around nervously and then when she realized where she was, she began to stretch her arms and legs. She unhooked her seatbelt and stood up to get her bag from the overhead compartment. She handed me my carry on and then we made our way down the aisle to the exit. We exited the terminal and made our way to baggage claim.

"Man Thing 1 I cannot wait until we get to the condo. I am so exhausted."

"Me too. That deal with the governor had me up so late last night."

"It had me up all night too. I'll be glad when we're done with this stuff forever. All of these sleepless nights and worrying about the repercussions of these deals are beginning to take a toll on me."

I rolled my eyes. Here she goes again. Every now and then Taylor would begin complaining about the job but here lately she had become increasingly negative. It was becoming annoying.

"Look, let's not focus on that this week. Let's just enjoy our week of fun in the sun and use this time to unwind."

Taylor sighed heavily but nodded her head in agreement. "Yeah you're right. Let's have some fun!"

We got our bags off of the conveyor belt and made our way towards the cellphone lot. When we got outside there was a man in a black suit standing in front of a black Suburban. He was holding a sign with both of our names written on it in big black letters. We waved at him and he immediately began to smile.

"Good afternoon ladies. I'm hoping you all had a wonderful flight. My name is Edwin and I'll be at your service for the duration of your stay."

"Thank you Edwin. If you don't mind, you can go ahead and take us to our condo."

"No problem."

We placed our bags in the trunk and got into the backseat of the car. I rolled the window down and took in the view of the palm trees as we made our way to South Beach. I loved driving past the big cruise ships and boats on the Port of Miami. It's something that we don't get to see everyday living in Indiana. Edwin got off on the exit that led to Alton Road. We continued along Alton Road until we finally pulled up at Continuum, where we would be staying for the week.

"Thank you so much Edwin. We probably won't be going anywhere else today but we'll give you a call if we do." I handed him a $100 bill and grabbed our bags from him. We wheeled our bags up to the security desk, grabbed the keys to our condo, walked to the elevator and headed to the 29th floor. When we made it up to the condo and unlocked the door, our exhausted mood immediately changed once we got inside. The condo was decorated with all white furniture and the floor to ceiling windows in the living room gave us a gorgeous view of the Atlantic Ocean. The kitchen had granite countertops and all stainless steel appliances and there was a basket of fruit and fancy chocolates waiting for us on the island in the middle of the room. We sat our bags down and went to check out the rest of the bedrooms. The first bedroom was decorated with black and white modern furniture and the king size bed sat in the far left corner of the room. There was an adjoining bathroom that was decked out with white and gray marble and modern his and hers sinks. There was a Jacuzzi tub and a standalone shower that had a marble bench inside and two detachable showerheads. We walked out of that room and down the hallway to the second bedroom. The second bedroom was decorated like the first one but it was a little bit bigger with a small chaise and end table next to the window. The bathroom was identical as well except instead of having two showerheads there was one rainfall showerhead and no marble bench inside the shower.

"You can have this room, Thing 1. I might meet a friend and put those two showerheads to good use while we're here," Taylor said and laughed.

I laughed and shook my head. "I should've known you were trying to come down here and be fast."

"Girl we are in Miami! I'm trying to get in all the trouble I can before we have to go back to Indy. Let's go to the pool."

"I thought you wanted to take a nap?"

"We can take a nap at the pool while we tan. Come on Thing 1! Quit being lame."

"Okay, okay, okay. I'll be ready in a few minutes."

While Taylor went to her room I dug through my luggage and located one of the six swimming suits that I brought with me. I laid the olive green bikini out on the bed and went through my bag of jewelry that I kept in my carry on and added a pair of gold hoops, a long gold body chain and a gold ankle bracelet. I stepped back to look at the outfit that I had created and decided that it looked good. I peeled off my t-shirt and leggings that I had worn just for the flight and made my way to the bathroom to take a shower. I turned the shower on and let the steady stream of the rainfall water beat against my body. I was careful not to get my hair wet because even though we were in Miami, I wanted my freshly styled pixie cut to last the entire week. After washing the filth of the plane off of my body I got out of the shower and dried off. I rubbed my body down with a mixture of body butter and sunscreen and put on my outfit that I had laid out on the bed. After looking at myself in the full-length mirror that was attached to the closet door, I decided to put on a little makeup to complete the look. It was way too hot outside for a full face but a little mascara, eyeshadow, bronzer and lip gloss immediately brightened my face up and I was ready to go. I grabbed my wallet, phone and the apartment keys and headed down the hallway to see if Taylor was ready. Taylor had brought a portable Bluetooth speaker with her and had reggae music playing while she was in the mirror winding her hips to the beat and doing her makeup. I snuck up behind her and began winding my hips against her and she started laughing.

"Look at you! You look good Thing 1."

"You look good too, Thing 2. I might need to borrow that swimsuit one day this week." Taylor had on a fuchsia bikini with a colorful sheer sarong tied around her waist.

"Now you know you can't fit all of that ass in this swimsuit." We both began to laugh. Taylor and I always joked about our physical differences; she was tall and slender while I was short and had more than enough hips and thighs for the both of us.

"Are you ready to go to the pool?"

Taylor added another layer of liquid lipstick to her lips and then flipped her hair around and put her braids into a big bun on top of her head. "I am now."

We made our way out of the apartment and back to the elevator and pressed the button for the penthouse level of the building. We figured the pool up there would be way less crowded than the one on the first floor attached to the lobby. As expected, there were only a few other people at the penthouse pool. We located two empty lounge chairs and while Taylor just sat her things down in the chair next to me, I laid my beach towel down on the chair and prepared to lie out. I put my sunglasses on and watched Taylor swim a couple of laps. I couldn't help but take in our surroundings and think about where we started. It seemed like just yesterday that we were just two naïve freshmen in college that were looking forward to retail jobs and college life. In my wildest dreams I never would've imagined that I could afford to live lavish in high-rise apartments and take random trips to Miami or travel abroad whenever I felt like it. After that crazy night at the club with Draya, Goldie had first hired us to make deliveries and pick up money all around Houston. We did that for a couple of months before he finally began to give us eight balls to sell at all of the parties on campus and any other club that Draya could sneak us into. We were so good that we would sell out of product before the parties would end. We never had to stand on a corner or do anything that we felt uncomfortable doing. We began bringing in more business than all of his other employees combined and Goldie definitely favored us for that. He's the one that gave us the nickname 'Thing 1 and Thing 2'. When we both turned 21 and graduated, Goldie gave us the idea of setting up a legitimate 'service based' business. He wanted to cater to a more expensive clientele but he knew it was a risky move and he couldn't have just anybody taking meetings and making deals with the elite. He needed people that were personable and could fit in in a boardroom and a ballroom. He needed people that were good with numbers and could keep track of large numbers of shipments and payments. He needed someone tech savvy who could set up this business and process payments without it being traced back to him or looking suspicious on tax records. In the end he decided what he needed, was Taylor and I.

30

Taylor interrupted my thoughts by splashing me with water. "Quit laying there being a diva and get in the pool!"

"I was trying to take a nap."

"Who comes to Miami to take a nap? Get in the pool."

I rolled my eyes behind my sunglasses but I stood up and stretched and removed my body chain. I walked over to the steps at the corner of the pool and walked down until the water was at my knees and sat down on the last step. The water was surprisingly warm. I sat there continuing to watch Taylor as she swam around me and tried to make me laugh by doing handstands and splashing water in my face.

"Alright now, don't get my hair wet."

"You're such a Debbie Downer. After we leave here do you want to go get something to eat and do a little shopping?"

"That's cool. What do you want to eat, seafood?"

"Now you know I want seafood. Do you want to go to A Fish Called Avalon?"

"I love that place. Let's go get dressed and try to beat the dinner crowd."

"Okay. If you don't mind I'm going to rent us a car. Edwin is great but you know I like to get up and go whenever I please without having to wait."

I laughed. "That's fine with me."

We got out of the pool and gathered our belongings from our chairs. Once we made it back to our room we both showered and dressed. We made our way down to the lobby where Edwin was already waiting to take us to pick up our rental car. I waited outside as Taylor went to talk to the attendant at the desk and paid for the car. A few minutes later she pulled up to me in a navy blue BMW 4 series convertible. I hopped in the car and we got on the highway and headed to the restaurant. Once we pulled up and parked, we noticed it wasn't very crowded at the tables outside so we told the hostess we wanted to eat out there. We ordered calamari and martinis as appetizers and enjoyed the view of the beach from our seats. When our drinks came Taylor raised her glass for a toast. "To continued success!" I tapped my glass against hers and took a sip of my martini.

"You know Thing 1 I never thought that my life would be like this."

"Neither did I, Thing 2. I definitely thought I was just going to be behind a desk coding for the rest of my life."

31

"Have you ever given any thought to what you're going to do when this is all over?"

"No, not really. I do know that all of this isn't going to last forever though."

"How would you feel about ending everything now?"

I stopped gazing out at the beach and turned my head to face Taylor. "Is there something wrong Taylor? What would make you ask that?"

"I've just been thinking about the future. That deal with the governor was very risky and if it hadn't worked out in our favor, we would've been in jail. Selling for Goldie in college was cool and the money is great but I think it's time for us to move on. After all, we're getting closer and closer to 30."

I sat there confused. Where was all of this coming from? Just a few seconds ago we were toasting to our success and now Taylor was saying she wanted out. Don't get me wrong; Taylor has never been a fan of the work we do and I understand why. Truly I do. But we were literally left with no choice. She was being ridiculous.

"I understand what you're saying but I don't think now is the right time for us to quit. We just signed a really big deal and it wouldn't be in our best interest to leave Goldie hanging at a time like this."

Taylor pursed her lips together. "I really don't care about leaving Goldie hanging. I've given that man more than enough of my life. My own family won't even talk to me because of this. Now I want to live on my own terms. Why are you always defending him?"

"I'm not defending him at all. I'm just trying to keep us alive. That's all I've ever tried to do is keep us alive."

"Well it's funny how every time you try to keep US alive you never consult ME. I didn't even want this life."

"I don't see you turning down any of the benefits that this life brings either. You didn't want out when we got on the plane. You didn't want out when you rented a BMW."

"Wow, really? Well I'm telling you now that I want out. I want more out of life than selling drugs and ducking and dodging the police."

"And I'm telling you that now is not a good time to get out. You can enjoy a boring life as a CPA or whatever you plan on doing later but right now we still have work to do."

Taylor opened her mouth to reply but our waitress came back over to take our order. We fixed our faces and plastered on fake smiles and put our dinner orders in. The rest of dinner was silent. I was fuming. I couldn't believe Taylor. Neither one of us had chosen this life but while we were in it, I was going to make the best of it. Taylor had always been opposed to working for Goldie but after she started to see how much money we were bringing in, she kept quiet. I had always felt bad about her parents not speaking to her after she told them where all of her money was coming from but she never brought them up so I assumed they were out of sight, out of mind. I guess tonight she had reached her breaking point. When our food came we both ate in silence. We finished dinner, paid the bill and left a tip, and rode back to the condo. When we got there Taylor went to her room and closed the door and turned her reggae music back on. That was fine with me. I didn't feel like talking anymore anyway. I went to my room and closed the door and laid across the bed and closed my eyes. Hopefully Taylor would be okay tomorrow. I wasn't going to let her attitude ruin the rest of my trip.

I woke up the next day to Taylor jumping up and down on my bed. "Wake up Thing 1! You've already slept through breakfast and you're not about to make me miss lunch too. Get up!"
She plopped down on me and began to tickle me. I immediately started kicking her off of me. I was extremely ticklish.
"Okay I'm up. I'm up! What are we doing today?"
"We're going shopping for sure. I was thinking we could rent some four wheelers and ride them up and down the beach too."
"Sounds like a plan. Let me get dressed."
Taylor left my room humming and dancing. I guess she was feeling better today. We never could be mad at each other for too long. I showered and put on some shorts and a t-shirt and my Gucci tennis shoes and headed to Taylor's room. Taylor was sitting on her bed texting someone but as soon as she seen me come in, she quickly put her phone away.
"New boo?"
"You know I always keep one or two around. You ready to go Thing 1?"
"Yes, let's go."
We decided to eat at The Front Porch Café since they served breakfast all day. We ate a hearty brunch and then headed to Bal Harbour Shops. A few hours and a few thousand dollars later, we loaded all of our shopping bags in the trunk of the car and headed to the beach. Before we got there we spotted an ATV rental place. We parked our car and went in to rent a few ATV's to ride. Since Taylor

---

had rented the car for the week, I decided to pick up the tab for the ATV's. After I had signed all of the paperwork for our rental and paid, the cashier asked us what color each of us wanted. I decided to go with red. I turned around to ask Taylor which color she wanted and she was preoccupied texting her new little boyfriend again. "Um, Earth to Taylor! Your new friend must have your nose wide open. Which color do you want?"

Taylor smiled and quickly put her phone in her back pocket. "Now you know to get me blue."

After a quick tutorial from the cashier, we began riding up and down the beach. We were having so much fun. At one point Taylor was going so fast that her ATV flipped over and I had to come and get her from the sand. We were both cracking up laughing as she shook the sand from her braids. We had only rented the ATV's for an hour so we made our way back to the rental place to turn them in once our time was up. We decided to get some dinner while we were out so we headed to The Big Pink. Since we had planned to go out later on and we knew we would be drinking, we kept it simple with burgers, fries and milkshakes.

"Where were you thinking of going tonight, Thing 1?"

"I'm not sure. We can do King of Diamonds. Or did you want to go to a regular club?"

"I was thinking of just going to a regular club and saving King of Diamonds for the weekend. How about Cameo?"

"Cameo is cool. We always have fun there."

We finished our food and then headed back to the condo. We both went to our rooms to get dressed and pregame before we hit the streets. I decided to keep it simple with a little black dress and gold accessories. As I was putting my makeup on, Taylor came in and passed me an already lit blunt. I took a couple of pulls and then handed it back to her.

"Okay then, Thing 1! You're looking like you're trying to bring somebody home tonight."

"Not at all. That's you looking like you're trying to cheat on your little friend that you've been texting all day."

Taylor's smile disappeared for a few seconds but she quickly recovered and started to laugh. "Please. He is just a friend, nothing more. You know love doesn't live here anymore. But go back to telling me how good I looked again," she said and spun around in a circle. She had on a purple Armani body con dress and matching

---

pink and purple Jimmy Choo heels that we had picked up from the mall earlier.

I laughed at her before I inhaled more smoke. "I can't stand you." We finished getting ready and headed out to the club. After we parked and walked up to Cameo we saw that there was a line outside of the club from the door to the end of the curb. We never wait in lines. We walked up to the front and I stood next to the bouncer. "Excuse me, how much is it for me and my friend to get in without standing in line?"

The bouncer looked down at me and I was already prepared with my eyelashes batted and the front of my dress pulled down a little lower so more of my breasts were showing. He smiled at me.

"Well you're looking so good I would love to let you in for free but Travis Scott is here tonight so skipping the line is going to run you $200 for you and your friend."

I smiled back at him and opened my clutch and peeled off twenty $20 bills. I peeled off another $100 and put it in his suit jacket pocket next to his handkerchief.

"Thank you. Make sure you get yourself a drink tonight and don't work too hard."

The bouncer unhooked the velvet rope that was blocking off the door. I grabbed Taylor's hand and led her through the doors while everyone still waiting in line yelled obscenities and insults towards us. As soon as we got into the club I tracked down a waitress and asked her how much it was to get a table in VIP. She told me a table was going to be $400. I opened my clutch and gave her the money and she led me up to the balcony where the VIP was located. As we were getting situated in our section, more waitresses came and took our orders for drinks and sat a tray of chocolate covered strawberries on the table. A couple of minutes later I could see the sparklers coming to bring us our bottles of champagne. After pouring our drinks, Taylor and I looked over the balcony and took in the atmosphere of the club. The lower level was already packed full of people and the VIP was filling up quickly. The DJ was playing all of the latest hip-hop music and everyone was dancing. No one was standing around. The energy in the club was high. We didn't know that Travis Scott was going to be there but he definitely brought all of Miami out to see him. Taylor and I danced with each other for a while until she told me she was going to the bathroom. As soon as she walked away, the DJ announced that Travis Scott was about to

---

take the stage. I wasn't really a huge fan so I took that time to sit on one of the couches in our section and rest my feet. I poured myself another drink and nodded my head to the beat of the song Travis was performing. While I was sitting there enjoying myself in my own little world, a man came and sat next to me, poured himself a drink and helped himself to some of our strawberries.

"Um, excuse me?"

"Oh I'm sorry. You were sitting over here looking lonely so I thought I would come and keep you company."

I gently grabbed the glass out of his hand and the napkin full of strawberries and placed them back on the table.

"I'm not lonely. I'm waiting on my friend to come back from the bathroom. You coming over, making that assumption and making yourself at home is very rude, by the way."

"My apologies, I didn't mean to offend you Baby Girl. I thought I was being a gentleman."

"You and I must have two different definitions of the word gentleman. Also…Baby Girl? Why not just ask me for my name?"

"Okay how about we start all over since I'm clearly doing everything wrong," he said and chuckled. It was then that I got a good look at his face. He was dark brown skinned with neatly groomed dreadlocks and a goatee. His locs were styled in an intricate bun. He had on a short sleeve gray dress shirt with a skinny yellow tie and gray dress slacks.

"My name is Rocky. What's your name?"

"My name is Fallon. What did your mother name you, Rocky?"

"Oh I don't give out my real name. Rocky will do for now."

I looked him up and down and smacked my lips. "It certainly will. Have a nice night, *Rocky*." I shifted my entire body away from him and faced the balcony so that my back was turned to him.

"Wow, really? I thought we were starting over? My real name is Desmond."

I turned my body back around towards him. "Was that so hard? It's nice to meet you Desmond. Why do they call you Rocky anyway?"

"Well…" He hesitated. "I used to have a little reputation when I was younger for knocking dudes out but I swear to you, that's all behind me now." I looked down and noticed all of the scars on his hands. He tried to hurry up and hide them. For some reason that made me smile.

"You shouldn't be ashamed of your scars. They're a part of what makes you, you."

He smiled at me with his brilliant white teeth. He was wearing a pair of snatch out gold teeth on the bottom row of his mouth. "Yeah, I guess you're right. So can I buy you a drink?"

I pointed at the bottles of champagne. "No thank you. I have more than enough liquor right here."

"I know you said that you were waiting on your friend to get back. This friend wouldn't be a boyfriend or anything, would they?"

"No, no boyfriend. I'm here in Miami with my best friend. She went to the bathroom."

"Oh okay. Are you just visiting Miami?" I nodded. "Where are you originally from?"

"I'm from Indianapolis, Indiana."

"Wow. It is a really small world. I'm the Social Media Director for the Indiana Pacers."

"Really? I worked with the owner on a business deal a couple of months ago."

"Oh yeah? What do you do?"

"I own my own consulting firm."

"What kind of consulting?"

"Um…Corporate Consulting. I provide resources to business owners that assure that they are always performing at the peak level."

"Wow. That sounds interesting. I might need your services one day."

"Maybe you will."

"So would it be too forward to ask for your number?"

"Yes it would. My first impression of you wasn't the greatest."

"Oh come on. I thought I had redeemed myself by now. I tell you what. I'll give you my number and you can decide whether or not you want to be bothered."

"I like that idea much better." I handed my phone over to him so he could type in his number.

"I'm only going to be in Miami for a few more days so I hope that you put that number to use."

"I'll think about it."

"Man…I thought I was wearing you down for a second there. I guess I thought wrong. I'll leave you alone. Can I at least take my strawberries with me?"

I laughed. "I guess you can since you've already got all of your germs on them."

He picked the napkin full of strawberries back up off of the table and stood up.

"It was nice to meet you Fallon. I hope you use that number." He walked away, shaking his head and smiling.

I stood up and looked over the balcony. Travis Scott was throwing open water bottles into the crowd and after he threw the last bottle he took a few steps back and then launched himself into the crowd. The crowd carried him around on their hands for a few seconds before security in the crowd led his body back towards the stage. It was pure pandemonium. I made a mental note to check out some of his music when I got back to the condo.

"Mmm hmm. You think you're slick."

I turned around to see that Taylor had made it back. "What are you talking about?"

"I saw you over here with that random dude whispering sweet nothings in your ear."

"Isn't he fine? He was rude but very nice to look at."

"Oh yes he was gorgeous. Did you give him your number?"

"No. I took his though."

Taylor shook his head and laughed. "You're always so difficult. Well my new friend is down there in the crowd so I'm going to go ahead and leave with him."

"What? Why didn't you bring him up here to introduce me to him?"

"You know security was acting stupid about him not having on a VIP wristband and wouldn't let him come up here."

"Oh yeah." I rolled my eyes. Club security is the worst. "Well text me and let me know that you made it to his place safely."

"Will do. Don't wait up. I'll probably just spend the night and come back to the condo in the morning…or the afternoon." She winked at me and handed me the keys to the rental.

"Okay well have fun. I love you Thing 2." I reached in to give her a hug goodbye.

"I love you too Thing 1."

I watched Taylor as she walked down the steps of VIP and maneuvered her way through the crowd to the entrance. I guess her friend was already waiting for her outside because I didn't see anyone walking with her or waiting at the door. I finished up my glass of champagne and decided to call it a night. I followed the same route that Taylor took to get out of the club and headed to the car. I hooked my phone up to the Bluetooth in the car and turned on my R&B playlist for the ride to the condo. When I made it to the condo I immediately took my heels off and started unzipping my dress to prepare to get in the shower. While I waited for the water to heat up I brushed my teeth to get the aftertaste of champagne out of my mouth. I checked my phone and had a text from Taylor.

Fontainebleau, Room 237. Don't wait up! 4:17 AM

I smiled at my screen and threw my phone back on the bed. I got in the shower and proceeded to lather my body with body wash. While I stood there and let the water and bubbles run down my body, I realized that I wouldn't mind a little company tonight either. I cut the water off and wrapped a towel around my body. I sat on the bed and grabbed my phone and began to scroll through my contacts. There wasn't any number saved under Desmond so I looked for Rocky. Nothing under that name either. I sat there confused because I know for a fact that I watched him put his number in my phone. Did he not press save? Just as I was about to say forget it and just go to sleep, I saw a contact in my phone that was named 'The Man of Your Dreams'. I smiled. He was so corny. I pressed *67 and then typed in his number. I laid back on the pillows as the phone rang.
"This is Desmond Peters."
"Wow. You're so formal at almost 5 in the morning."
"Who is this?"
"It's the woman of your dreams. I hope you enjoyed your strawberries."
He was silent for a few seconds and then he began to chuckle.
"Fallon...I'm glad you decided to use my number. What are you still doing up?"
"I just got out of the shower. I might call it a night but that depends on you."
"Why does that depend on me?"
"It depends on how fast you can get over here and pick me up. Or were you in for the night?"
"Give me a few minutes to get dressed and I'll come and get you. Where am I coming to?"
"100 South Pointe Drive."
"Okay. I'll see you in a few. Don't go to sleep on me and have me out there looking stupid."
I laughed. "I promise I won't. I'm wide awake."

—

I hung up the phone and began to get dressed. I looked through all of the clothes in my suitcase and decided to slip on a maxi dress, sans underwear. There was no telling what this night would lead to so I had to be prepared. I waited 15 minutes and pressed *67 and called Desmond's number again.

"Hey, are you on your way?"

"I've been outside for like 5 minutes. You know, this would be a lot easier if you would just give me your number."

"It would be, wouldn't it? I'm on my way down now. What kind of car are you in?"

"A white Range Rover."

"Okay. Here I come."

I grabbed my wallet, keys and phone and made my way down to his car. When I got down to the truck Desmond was standing outside next to the passenger door. He had changed out of his club attire and had on a white V-neck t-shirt, black basketball shorts and black and white Nike slides.

"Your chariot awaits, my dear," he said as he opened the door for me.

I laughed. "Well aren't you sweet? Thank you."

Once I was in the car he closed the door and jogged around the front and got in on the driver side.

"I was surprised you really called me."

"I was surprised too. You didn't leave me with the best first impression."

"I admit it; I did kind of crash and burn before. So where are we going?"

"I don't know. What is there to do this late? Or this early?"

"Nothing really. Are you hungry? We can go get some breakfast."

"No. I'm not really in a breakfast mood. I tell you what…how about we go to the beach and listen to the waves?"

"That sounds good to me. Let me stop at Wal-Mart or something and get us some blankets to sit on."

He grabbed his phone and asked Siri for the nearest Wal-Mart and luckily, there was one three minutes away from where we were. We pulled up and parked.

"I'm going to run in and get the blankets. Do you want any snacks?"

"Yes, you can just bring me lemonade and some chips or something."

He got out and walked into the entrance of the store. When he walked out of my view, I quickly got out of the car and took a picture of his license plate. It was probably a rental, but I still wanted to be safe. I sent the picture to Taylor.

Hey Thing 2. You're probably busy right now but I'm with the dude from the club. Here's his license plate if you don't hear from me tomorrow. 5:38 AM

Ten minutes or so passed before Desmond came out with two bags full of blankets and snacks. He pulled out of the parking lot and we headed to the beach. We found a parking spot and then walked down a sandy hill and set up camp a little ways away from the hill. Desmond laid the blankets out and we both sat down. We sat there in silence for a while just watching and listening to the waves crash. There was a half moon and it was so dark that you couldn't see where the sky ended and the sea began. Desmond was the first to break the silence.

"So Fallon…what's your story?"

"There's not really much to tell. I run a business with my best friend and that consumes most of my time. No man, no kids, no pets."

"So you're all about making money, huh?"

"That's not what I'm all about. It's just the only thing that makes sense right now. What about you? What's your story?"

"Well I was born and raised here in Miami, Carol City to be exact. I went to college on a football scholarship at Vanderbilt University, majored in Marketing, became interested in digital marketing and when I seen that the NFL wasn't in my future, that's what I focused on. I've been with the Pacers now for 2 years. I don't really know anybody in Indy so work consumes my life too. I try to come back home to Miami as much as I can. I still have a lot of family here."

"I've been trying to place your accent all night long. I didn't think you were from here."

"Yeah, born and raised in the county of Dade," he said and we both laughed at him quoting the popular Trick Daddy song. "I'm Haitian so that explains the accent. Is your family still in Indy?"

I nodded. "I don't really have much family but the ones I do have are there. We're not very close. My parents died when I was younger."

—
41

"I'm sorry to hear that." An awkward silence fell over us and we went back to watching the waves. I decided to break the silence this time.

"You know, now that you know me you can take a break from work and let me show you around the city once we both get back."

"How can I do that? You won't even let me have your number."

We both laughed. "Listen, in my line of work I can never be too careful. You could be crazy and I don't have time to get stalked right now."

"Little ol' me? Do I look crazy?"

I tilted my head and squinted my eyes at him. "Do you want the real answer or do you want me to lie?"

"Wow," he said as he chuckled to himself. "That's cold. No seriously though, I'm harmless. You should give me a chance."

"We'll see."

I went back to watching the waves. I opened the bottle of lemonade that he bought me and took a sip. The coolness of the lemonade immediately sent a chill through my body and I began to shiver.

"Are you cold? Here. Let's rearrange this really quick."

He stood up and picked up his blanket. After he shook the sand off of it, he joined me on my blanket and wrapped his blanket around my shoulders.

"Thank you."

"No problem. See, I'm a good guy."

I shook my head and smiled. "Yeah, yeah, yeah. Like I said, we'll see about that."

He ignored my attitude and took the opportunity to wrap his arm around me. I thought about moving it but I didn't. It felt good to get some attention from someone with testosterone for a change.

"Hey guys! Guys! You can't be out here sleep. There's no sleeping on the beach."

I opened my eyes and was immediately blinded by the sun. Desmond and I sat up and acknowledged the policeman that had just woke us up. Apparently we had dozed off and fell asleep on the beach.

"Sorry about that officer. We'll be on our way in just a second."

We gathered up the blankets and the trash from our snacks and headed back to his truck. I checked my phone while we walked. It was almost noon. I had a text from Taylor.

—

Smh, see I knew you were trying to be fast, lol. Have fun! 9:02 AM

Desmond unlocked the doors and opened mine again so that I could get in. Once he got in the car he pulled out of the parking spot and made his way towards the freeway to take me back to my condo.
"I can't believe we fell asleep on the beach," I said as I stretched my arms out.
"I can. I wrapped these strong arms around you and you almost melted. You snore extremely loud, by the way."
I laughed and softly punched his arm. "No I don't. You're so extra."
A few minutes later we pulled up in front of the condo.
"Well Fallon, it's been a pleasure getting to spend some time with you. Can I have your number now?"
"Thank you for taking me to the beach. No you can't," I said as I opened the door and closed it behind me. Desmond rolled the window down.
"Really? I was a perfect gentleman last night. How am I going to get in touch with you?"
"Look, last night was great but I told you, I can never be too careful. You're in Indy; I'm in Indy. When you get back in town, figure out how to find me."
I walked into the building, but not before catching a glimpse of Desmond staring at me, shaking his head and smiling before he pulled off.

Chapter 4

"Well would you look at what the cat drug in? I thought you had moved out on me."

Archie met me at the entrance of my apartment building wearing a huge smile. He helped me with my bags to the elevator. I was really happy to see him too.

"Now Archie, you know I would never move out without saying goodbye first. I just took a little vacation to Miami for a week."

"Ooh, Miami. I have some stories about that place right there! Why, I remember back in 1963 the misses and I took a little vacation there and, well, let's just say nine months later my son Junior was born." We both began to laugh. "Well Archie I would love to tell you all about my trip but I'm a little tired from the plane ride so I'm going to go ahead and head upstairs."

"Oh yeah, I know how you feel. That jet lag is nothing to play with. You go ahead and get you some rest and I'll see you in the morning."

"Okay Archie, see you tomorrow."

I got on the elevator and pressed my head back against the wall of the elevator until it stopped on my floor. The rest of the week in Miami was a blur. Taylor and I shopped until we dropped, rode jet skis, went parasailing, swam with dolphins and of course, partied like there was no tomorrow. I was extremely exhausted. The doors of the elevator opened and I dragged my luggage to my front door and walked inside. The smell of the vanilla plug in's that I had placed all over my apartment immediately filled my nose. I was so happy to be back in my own home and my own space. I opened my suitcase and immediately put all of the clothes in my dirty clothes hamper and put all of my jewelry, shoes and toiletries back where they went. I didn't feel like dealing with them in the morning so it was better to put everything away now. I went to my bathroom and turned the shower on. I looked in the mirror while I waited for the water to heat up. My hair was a mess after jet skiing so I had put some quick finger waves in so that I wouldn't look crazy for the rest of the week. They were still holding on strong. I got in the shower and washed up. I got out and rubbed body butter all over my body. I took the terry cloth bathrobe hanging on the back of my bathroom door and put it on. I plopped down on my bed and grabbed my iPad that I kept on my nightstand. I opened my emails and immediately regretted it. There were 371 emails waiting for me in my inbox. Instantly annoyed, I shut down my iPad and decided that I was going to call it a night. The sun hadn't even gone down yet but I was exhausted. I set my alarm for six in the morning and put my phone on Do Not Disturb. I turned on my TV and switched the channel to HBO. A rerun of the last episode of Game of Thrones was coming on. I was snoring before the opening credits ended.

The next morning I walked into the building where our office was located and headed to the elevators. Once inside, I pressed the number 15 and headed up to our office. The elevator doors opened and the glass doors that had Smith & Scott Consulting in large white translucent letters on the front immediately met me. I walked through them and greeted our receptionist, Kayla, who was up making herself a cup of coffee and swaying to the rap music that was playing from her computer.

"Good Morning Kayla."

She spun around and almost spilled the piping hot coffee all over herself. She put the cup down and rushed over to the computer to turn the music off.

"Good morning Ms. Scott. I'm sorry about the music. I had gotten here a little early to answer emails after our week off and I guess I lost track of time."

"I don't mind the music. Just turn it down a little and make sure to turn it off if someone comes in. How was your vacation?"

"It was great! I went to Chicago for the week with my boyfriend. We had so much fun. How was your vacation, Ms. Scott?"

I chuckled. "Kayla, call me Fallon. I may be your boss but we don't have to be so formal. I'm not that much older than you. Taylor and I had a great time in Miami. Speaking of her, is she here yet?"

"Yes, she's back in her office. Oh, and I cleared the voicemail box this morning. Here are all of the messages for you," she said and handed me a stack of post-its with names and numbers written on them.

I skimmed through the post-its and let out a heavy sigh. "Well I guess I'll go ahead and get to work. I'll be in my office if you need me."

I opened the glass door that separated the reception area from our offices in the back and walked down the hallway. I stopped at Taylor's office and softly knocked on the door. Taylor had been looking at her phone but immediately stopped when I knocked.

"Hey Thing 1. What's up?"

"Nothing much, just got to the office. Planning a fun filled day of catching up on all of these calls and emails," I said as I waved the pile of post-its in the air.

Taylor laughed and picked up her own pile of post-its that had been sitting on her desk. "Yeah it looks like that for me too. I guess I don't even have to warn you about your inbox."

I rolled my eyes. "Yeah, I made the mistake of logging in last night so I already know what's waiting for me in there. I'll let you get back to work."

"Okay. Let me know when you're ready to go to lunch."

"Will do."

I continued down the hallway and walked into my office. I sat my purse down on my desk and plopped down on my desk chair. I absolutely loved our office space. Although everyone had their own office and own space, everything was glass so I could easily look to my left and see Taylor in her office or look to my right and see Kayla up at her desk. We could always see who was coming or going so there was never any surprises. We didn't keep product in the office but you could never be too careful. Because our office was in the corner of the building, we had more than enough privacy from the other businesses that rented a space. I logged onto my computer and reluctantly opened my email inbox. There were even more emails than when I checked last night. I sighed and scrolled down to the last read message and began reading, answering, and deleting the messages. Luckily for me it was a lot of thank you notes from

—

current clients, including one from Governor Pearson who had received his first shipment without any issues. There were a lot of inquiries for new business that I marked unread. Taylor and I liked to go through those together to make sure the inquiries were legit and if they were from people that we actually wanted as clients. We received a lot of inquiries from people that had received our card from friends and colleagues. Word tends to get around quickly in these types of social circles and our demand was always high because we kept our product pure, no cutting required. To weed out the riff raff, if they weren't in the tax bracket that we catered to, we always passed. After an hour or so I had finally completed clearing out my inbox so I got started on the phone messages. Thankfully, I got the voicemail for many of the calls and requested that they call me back. As I was finishing up the phone calls I noticed a deliveryman walking in with a large bouquet of roses. I automatically assumed that they were from Kayla's boyfriend or from whomever Taylor was dealing with that week. I went back to making my phone calls. A few minutes later, I watched as Kayla picked up the bouquet and began walking towards…my office? I was confused.

"Fallon, these are for you. Who do you have sending you flowers up here?" Kayla had the biggest grin on her face.

"I don't know who those are from. Did they come with a card?"

"Ooh, you're doing it like that? You and Taylor are goals, for real! Wait a second…okay, here's the card." She handed the small white envelope over to me. I opened it and read the messy handwriting.

I found you. Call Me.

I stood there puzzled for a second and then it finally clicked. I tried to suppress my smile because Kayla was still standing there looking as confused as I just was.

"Fallon? Do you want me to send the flowers back?"

"No that's okay. I know who sent them. Thank you for bringing them to me."

Kayla sat the bouquet on the edge of my desk and then excused herself and walked back to the front. I watched her the entire time and once she was back in her seat, I quickly grabbed my cellphone and scrolled through my contacts until I landed on the name 'The Man of Your Dreams'.

"This is Desmond Peters."

"How did you know I liked roses?"

"Well, well, well…I guess I did something right because you didn't call me private, Ms. Fallon."

"Yeah well, if you already know where I work, calling you private would be a bit redundant. How did you find me anyway?"

"I know people in high places. Isn't that who your company caters to?"

"Correct. So you found me. Now what?"

Desmond chuckled. "Well now that you're not being so difficult, I was hoping I could get to know you better."

"Look Desmond, you're a nice guy and everything but I really don't have time for any distractions right now."

"Wow. I'm a distraction? I think that hurts worse than an actual insult." We both laughed.

"I know you're a busy woman but how about we go to dinner tonight so that you can insult me in person. I'd love to see you again."

"Hmmm…I don't know…"

"Fallon don't make me beg. I'm not too proud to but I really didn't plan on begging for a dinner date this morning so I'm a bit rusty. Do I have to sing? That's it. I have to sing to you," he said and began to clear his throat.

"Whew, please don't," I said in between my laughter. "Okay let's do dinner tonight. When and where?"

"How about Morton's? Is 7 o'clock a good time?"

"7 o'clock is perfect. I'll meet you there."

Desmond began to laugh. "Here I was thinking I was really making progress and you won't even let me be a gentleman and come pick you up."

"You got my number today. Let's not push it on the blessings." We both laughed.

"Alright well, I will see you at 7 then beautiful."

"See you then," I said as I hung up.

I'm not going to lie; I was a little excited to see Desmond again. We had a really good time on the beach in Miami. It would be nice to actually go on a real date with him and not just a late night rendezvous.

"Excuse me? Where did these flowers come from and who has you in here cheesing like a Cheshire cat?" I must have been smiling a little too big while I was in my daze because I didn't even notice

—

48

Taylor standing in front of my desk and running her fingers over the petals of the roses.

"Remember the guy you seen me speaking to at Cameo?"

Taylor stood there with a blank face for a moment and then a sly smile crept across her face. "Yeah I remember him. How'd he find you all the way up here in Indy?"

"He lives here too. He works for the Pacers."

"Shut up! See if he can get us tickets to a game!"

I laughed. "I have to go on the date first before I start asking him to take advantage of the perks of his job."

"Please. If he went through all of the trouble to look you up and send you flowers to your job then you are already in there. Are you ready to go to lunch?"

"Yes I am. Let me send this last email and then I'll meet you at Kayla's desk."

I finished typing out the email and then hit send. I locked the screen on my computer, grabbed my purse, and then headed up to the reception area where Taylor was talking and laughing with Kayla.

"You ready to go Thing 2?"

"Yes girl lets go. I am starving!"

"Kayla, do you want to join us?"

"No thank you. My boyfriend is bringing me something to eat."

"Okay well…we'll see you in about an hour."

We both walked to the elevator and took it down to the lobby of the building. Our office was right in the heart of downtown Indy so anywhere that we wanted to eat was within walking distance. We decided to go to one of our favorite spots named Scotty's Brewhouse. We made excellent timing because right when we put our orders in and sat down, groups of people began coming in for the lunchtime rush. Once our order was up, I brought both of our trays over and we sat at a booth close to the door.

"So…are you excited about your date?"

"I don't know. It's just another night for me."

Taylor rolled her eyes. "Yeah right. Another night for you would be lying up in that apartment watching Netflix. What are you going to wear?"

"I haven't really thought about it. I'm not dressing up, that's for sure."

"What do you mean you're not going to dress up?"

"It's not like this is our first time hanging out. He's taking me to Morton's and trying to impress me. You know I'm not easily impressed, especially not with expensive steakhouses. I don't even eat steak."

"Well I hope you go in there and act like you've got some sense. My husband could be sitting courtside waiting on me when we get those tickets." We both began to laugh. After we finished our lunch, we slowly headed back to the office. The rest of the day ran smoothly and at exactly 5 o'clock, I logged out of my computer and began to leave. As I walked down the hallway, Taylor was talking on her office phone but placed the call on hold and yelled out, "Have fun! Remember my courtside tickets!"

I waved goodbye as I laughed and yelled back, "I promise!"

Rush hour traffic was terrible as usual but I made it home in enough time to take a shower and get dressed. I sat there for a while looking through my closet and putting different outfits together but nothing seemed to look right. I finally decided on a pair of jeans and a nice blouse with some heels. I did my makeup and freshened up my hair and then finally got dressed. I grabbed my purse and my phone and then headed back down to my car. I made the ten-minute drive back downtown and pulled into the restaurant parking lot. I walked inside and before I could even say anything to the host she greeted me with, "Are you Fallon Scott?"

My stomach dropped. "Yes ma'am, I am."

"Oh great, Mr. Peters has booked the private dining room for you two. Follow me."

I exhaled with relief. I should've known he was going to try to go all out for tonight. The host led me to the dining room in the back. The room was very dimly lit and there were wine bottles that lined the walls. They had removed all of the other tables in the room except for one in the middle of the floor with one single candle lit on the tabletop. I could see Desmond standing beside the table holding a bouquet of roses. He was dressed in a white short-sleeved shirt, a red skinny tie and some navy blue slacks with brown loafers. He had taken the bun in his hair down and his hair hung freely past his chest. When he seen me walk in he immediately began to smile. The host set our menus down on the table as Desmond pulled my chair out for me to take a seat.

"I must say you are even more beautiful than I remembered."

"Thank you. You look very handsome as well. How was your day today?"

"It was a typical day, nothing too exciting. It's a lot brighter now that you're here."

"Desmond, stop trying to make me blush."

"Is it working?"

"Absolutely not." We both laughed.

Our waiter came over and took our drink orders. Desmond ordered us a bottle of wine and we put in our dinner orders.

"So tell me a little bit more about your business."

"There's not really much to tell. I provide business owners with resources that-"

"Yeah I know, you told me that but what does that mean? I checked out your website when I was trying to track you down and it was very vague as well."

I shrugged my shoulders. "If you went to our website and looked at the content and didn't have an understanding of the company after that then perhaps our services just aren't for you."

Desmond stared at me with a blank face. This is why I didn't really date. I didn't have time for all of these 'get to know you' questions. As far as I was concerned, everyone I encountered was the police. I could sense Desmond was getting a little irritated so before I shut down completely, I decided to try and break the ice and save the date.

"So…how was it growing up in Miami? I don't think I could ever leave a place as beautiful as that."

Desmond chuckled. "Yeah well, not every place in Miami is as beautiful as downtown or South Beach. That's all for show for the tourists. If you ever want to see the real Miami let me know. I'll give you a tour."

"Can I ask you something?"

"You can ask me anything."

I placed my hand on his and began tracing the scars. "Were you really well known for knocking people out?" We both laughed. Desmond removed his hand from mine and began to examine the scars.

"I was but that's all in the past. Where I grew up was pretty rough. It was either knock them out or get knocked out. You know I look to good to be out here getting knocked out." He rubbed his beard and smiled.

—

I rolled my eyes and laughed. "You look alright."

"Just alright?"

"Mediocre at best."

Desmond grabbed his chest. "You sure know how to break a man's heart. It's cool though. I know you like me."

"Oh yeah? How do you know that?"

"Because after getting to know you a little, I know that if you didn't like me you wouldn't be here."

I raised my wine glass and tilted my head. "Here's to you making good observations."

Desmond reached out and grabbed my hand and stared me in eyes. "No seriously though Fallon, you don't have to be so guarded and uptight with me. I'm a good guy. I don't mean you any harm. I know I came off a little arrogant in the beginning but I think you'll really like me if you get to know me."

"We'll see. I will say I like what I know so far."

Desmonds' face lit up and he began to smile. The waiter came back and set our orders on the table. We ate our food in silence. It was very awkward. After we finished our food the waiter came back and asked if we would like any dessert. We both declined. After he paid the bill and left a tip, he walked me outside to my car.

"Wow. This is nice. What is this, the C-class coupe?"

"Um, no sweetie. This is the E-class coupe."

Desmond put his hand against his chest. "Excuse me. I didn't mean to make it seem like you were broke." We both laughed.

"Where did you park?"

"Oh I didn't drive tonight. I took an Uber. I don't live too far from here."

"So how were you going to get home?"

"I was just going to call another Uber."

"What? No you're not. Come on and get in. I'll take you home."

"It's really not that far. It'd only be like a $5 trip."

"If it's really not that far then quit being difficult and let me take you home. I'm being nice to you for a change; you should take advantage of it."

Desmond laughed. "Okay, okay. You win."

He walked over to the passenger side and let himself in. I pulled out of the parking lot and joined the busy downtown traffic. Desmond did a great job of giving me turn-by-turn directions to his apartment, which wasn't very far from the restaurant like he had said previously. His building was right next to Bankers Life Fieldhouse. "Wow. This is super convenient for you to get to work in the morning."

"Yeah, that's one of the reasons why I picked this place."

"You walk to work every day?"

"Every single day."

"Even in the winter?"

"In the winter I cry and walk at the same time."

We both laughed and I found a spot in the parking garage attached to the building. I expected for Desmond to get out of the car but he just sat there.

"So…I know this may be too forward of me, but would you like to come upstairs for a second? You don't have to stay long if you don't want to."

"Well…" I hesitated. I wasn't ready for the date to be over just yet but I couldn't afford to get caught with my guard down.

"It's cool if you don't. I just wanted to spend a little more time with you."

"Okay. I'll come up. Don't try to kill me or anything. I've already text your address to my best friend and the police are on speed dial." Desmond put both of his hands up and smiled. "I'll be on my best behavior. I promise."

He got out and walked over to the driver's side of the car and helped me out. We walked to the garage elevator and Desmond reached out and pressed the number four. The elevator was old and rusty so the ride up was extremely bumpy and unsettling. When the doors opened Desmond led the way to his door. He opened the door and turned on the closest light switch and then with a very Vanna White-esque wave of his hand, he said, "Welcome to my humble abode."

His apartment was a large loft and was decorated with black and tan modern furniture. There were hardwood floors throughout and black appliances. It was your typical bachelor pad; he had every kind of electronic device known to man but it was very clean.

"Make yourself at home."

I took my shoes off and left them near the door and began to walk around and give myself a tour. The black and tan theme was everywhere; he had a small black dining room set with tan cushions on the chairs, black and tan bar stools, and in the half bathroom there were black and tan towels and rugs.

"You have a very nice place. Do you mind if I take a look upstairs?"

"Sure."

I walked up the steps and was immediately met by his king sized platform bed. The bed was too big for the loft space but there wasn't any other furniture so it didn't look cluttered. I looked over the balcony down at Desmond who was standing in front of the enormous TV going through the channel guide. I made my way back down the steps and took a seat on the couch.

"This TV is huge. What size is that, 62?"

"Close. Its 75."

"You're going to go blind."

"I doubt it but it's cute that you're worried about my pupils." I threw one of the pillows on the couch at him and he quickly ducked to dodge it. He quit flipping through the channels and turned the TV onto ESPN. He set the remote down on the coffee table and joined me on the couch.

"Why are you all the way over there?"

"I'm sorry. I was just trying to be a gentleman."

"I don't mind you sitting next to me. Just don't try to kill me."

Desmond laughed and we both switched positions on the couch. I put my legs up on the couch and laid back against the pillows while he laid back in between my legs. His long locs had a mind of their own and were sprawled every which way on my thighs. I picked up a few strands and began to play with them while he watched Sports Center.

"Are you comfortable? Do you want anything to drink?"

"No, I'm fine like this."

"Okay I'm just checking. I always want you to feel comfortable with me."

"I do feel comfortable with you. I haven't felt comfortable like this in a long time."

"Really? When was your last relationship?"

"I haven't been in a relationship since college."

"That long ago? What happened with that?"

"Um…" I hesitated. "Let's just say work got in the way."

"I understand that completely. Would you be open to getting in another one?"

"Honestly? I wouldn't mind being with someone but they would have to be understanding of my lifestyle and my career. What about you?"

"I haven't been in a relationship in a couple of years. Nothing bad happened, it just didn't work out. I haven't really found anybody that I've liked since then. A lot of one night stands but nothing real though. Not until now." He looked up at me and smiled. I stared back at him, emotionless.

"You really think you would want to be in a relationship with me?"

"Fallon you're beautiful, you're ambitious, and you're driven. You're not fazed by my job or who I work for. Who wouldn't want to get to know you and hope it turns into something more?"

I finally smiled. "You're doing it again."

"Doing what?"

"That thing where you try to make me blush."

"Is it working?"

"Maybe. Maybe not."

Desmond looked up at me and shook his head and smiled. He went back to watching TV and I sat there consumed with my own thoughts. He was a really great guy. I'm typically not very trusting of people but he did make me feel comfortable and except for that initial encounter in Cameo, he had been a perfect gentleman. Not to mention, I hadn't talked to anyone or been with anyone since Xavier in college. I was well overdue for some companionship and affection.

"Well Desmond it's getting kind of late so…"

"Yeah you're right. I wish you could stay longer but I understand. Here, I'll walk you out."

He got up and walked towards the door. When he turned around, to his surprise, I was at the bottom of the steps and had already taken my shirt off.

"I didn't mean I was leaving. I meant it's getting late so we should head to bed," I said as I unbuttoned my pants and pulled them down. Desmond sat there and stared at me for a few moments before moving from the door and walking over towards me at the steps.

"Are you serious?"

I turned around and walked slowly up the steps. When I got to the top I threw my panties and bra down at him.

"Are you coming up or not?"

Chapter 5

"Hey Fallon, I'm about to head out but I wanted to drop off your tickets for the Holiday Ball tonight."

I looked up from typing on my computer to see Kayla placing a white envelope on my desk. I grabbed the envelope from her and pulled out the tickets inside. Governor Pearson had invited us to the Democratic Holiday Ball tonight as a thank you for our services.

"Thank you Kayla. There are three tickets in here. Are you sure you don't want to go?"

"No thank you. I'm not very good at working the room at fancy parties. I'm sure you guys will have a great time though. Besides, I know you probably wanted to bring *Desmond* instead," she said and sighed. She put the back of her hand on her forehead and acted like she was fainting while fanning herself with the other hand. I tilted my head and smirked at her.

"Alright now. Don't make me call your boyfriend and tell him you have eyes for somebody else."

Kayla laughed. "Okay, okay. I quit. But girl, that man is so fine! He has me blushing and stuttering every time he comes in here for you."

"Meh...he looks alright I guess," I said and shrugged my shoulders.

"He looks alright? Girl...lets trade then!" We both laughed and Kayla said goodbye again while walking out of the office. It had been about four months since Desmond and I went on our first official date and since then, he had become a regular visitor at our office to bring me lunch or just work on his laptop while I worked. Both Kayla and Taylor all but drooled every time he came in. When Kayla initially passed on going to the Ball, I asked Desmond if he would be my date and he happily obliged. Taylor was bringing a date as well. I looked at the clock on my computer and it was well after 5 o'clock. I rushed to log out of my computer and gathered my things to head home. I needed enough time to do my hair and

---

makeup and get dressed because the Ball started at 7. I sped all the way home. It was a wonder that I didn't get pulled over. By the time I got home, I had a little over 45 minutes to get everything done so of course I was frantic and rushing around. I had just slipped my dress on when the buzzer at my door began to ring.

"Yes, Archie?"

"Ms. Scott, Mr. Peters is down here waiting for you."

"Okay thank you. I'm on my way down."

I slipped on my shoes and then took one last look at myself in the mirror. I had bought a floor length, cap sleeve, emerald green gown. I opened my closet and pulled out my brown mink stole and headed downstairs. When I got down to the lobby I could see Desmond looking extremely handsome in a black tuxedo with an emerald green bow tie and cummerbund. He and Archie looked like they were engaged in a pretty heated debate.

"Oh come on man! The only reason why they won is because the Cowboys didn't make it out of the playoffs. With Dak, Dez and Zeke on their roster, there's no way they shouldn't win this year!"

Archie shook his head. "The Patriots would've won with or without the Cowboys being there. They've got a nice squad, young blood. You have to give Tom Brady his props."

"I will never give him his props. If we didn't have Tony Romo making us look bad for all of those years we wouldn't even be having this conversation."

I cleared my throat. "I don't mean to interrupt but we're going to be late if you guys keep arguing sports."

Archie and Desmond both turned around and smiled. Desmond walked over and extended his hand so that I could spin in a circle. "You look beautiful, Fallon."

"Doesn't she? I already told her that if you ever mess up she could go ahead and come home with me. I'm sure my wife wouldn't mind."

All of us laughed. "Trust me; I'm not going to mess up any time soon," Desmond said and pulled me closer to kiss me on my forehead.

"Alright you two, you guys can settle this debate later but we really have to go. We'll see you later Archie."

"You two have a good time tonight and don't stay out too late."

We both laughed. Archie was old enough to be our dad so we were used to the playful scolding. "I promise you we won't."

———

Desmond opened the door for me and I walked out to the limo that was waiting for us. Desmond waited until the train of my dress was all the way inside before he slid into the backseat with me.

"Thank you for coming out with me tonight."

"You know I wasn't going to miss a night out with you. I also wasn't going to miss an opportunity to look this fly," he said as he brushed off the sleeves of his tux.

"Must you be so dramatic?" I shook my head while laughing.

"Don't act like you don't like it."

The limo driver put the partition down to let us know that we were pulling up the Ball. It was being held at the J.W. Marriott. When I looked out of the window I could see an assortment of tuxedos and ball gowns walking in, ready to partake in the affair. The driver dropped us off right in front of the hotel entrance and Desmond helped me out of the car. Two men were sitting at a tablecloth-covered table full of cards right inside the entrance.

"Good evening gentlemen. I'm Fallon Scott of Smith & Scott Consulting and this is my guest."

One of the men scanned a list of names on a clipboard until he found mine while the other searched through the cards on the tabletop.

"Ah, here you are. You will be seated at table nine. You all enjoy your evening."

He handed me a white card that had both of our names on it with the number nine printed in metallic gold ink. We walked into the ballroom and were amazed at the decorations. It truly looked like a winter wonderland in there. There were round tables arranged on both sides of the floor while the middle was clear and reserved for the dance floor. At the front of the room there was a podium and a microphone and a five-piece band that had already began playing mid-tempo tunes. We walked to the left side of the room and searched for our table. Our table was right in the middle of the row of tables aligning the wall. Taylor and her date were already sitting there along with two other couples that didn't look familiar to me.

"Well look who decided to finally show up. Hey ya'll!"

I smirked at Taylor's smart comment. "Well nobody told you to get here when they first opened the doors. Hello, I'm Fallon and this is Desmond," I said as I extended my hand across Taylor towards her date. Desmond simply nodded his head towards him.

"It's very nice to meet you Fallon. I've heard a lot about you. My name is Brent." Brent shook my hand and then placed his arm around Taylors' shoulders. He was brown skinned with a clean-cut baldhead, no facial hair and the longest lashes I've ever seen on a man. Taylor had on a red sequined gown and Brent had on a black tuxedo with a red bowtie. Desmond pulled out my seat and helped me with my dress as I sat down. As soon as he was seated next to me, I tapped Taylor under the table and leaned over.

"Where did he come from?" I whispered.

"Tinder. You know how I do."

"Good job. He's gorgeous."

"Yeah I know," she said as she dramatically flipped her braids over her shoulder. We both giggled. Right as I was about to joke around some more, a man approached the podium at the front and announced that dinner would be served shortly. Both Desmond and I focused our attention on the menus that were placed on the decorative tablecloth. The first course would be a Caesar salad or loaded potato soup with our choice of filet mignon with asparagus or lobster tail with mixed vegetables for the entrée. For dessert there was a choice of a chocolate molten lava cake or cheesecake. There was also an open bar. The servers came over and took our menu cards and shortly after, we were told to stand for the arrival of Governor Pearson and his date. They were met with a standing ovation from the room. As they took their seats, I noticed Mitch Walters, the owner of the Pacers and his wife sitting directly across the room from us. I nudged Desmond with my elbow.

"Look. There's Mitch."

Desmond looked in the direction I was pointing. "Mitch? Mitch who?"

"Mitch Walters."

"Who is that?"

I looked at him, confused. "Mitch Walters is the owner of the Pacers. You don't know your own boss?"

Desmond looked dumbfounded for a second and then quickly fixed his face and began to laugh. "Of course I know my boss. I refer to him as Mr. Walters so much that I forgot that his first name was Mitch."

I put on a fake smile but I wasn't buying it. He genuinely didn't know who he was. That was odd to me but I decided not to make a big deal about it. The servers came back over and began serving us our soup and salads. While we ate we got to know the other two couples seated at the table with us. One of them was the CEO of

Allison Transmission, while the other was a board member for Roche Diagnostics. I gave Taylor a look that she knew all too well and she nodded back at me. I proceeded to give them our general elevator pitch while Taylor reached into her clutch and provided them with our business cards. Unbeknownst to Desmond and Brent, we weren't really there to just have a good time with the governor; there was big money in the room and we were looking to add to our client list. The servers came and cleared our salad plates away and quickly replaced them with our entrée choices. The entire table fell silent as we all dug into our meals. I made a note to get the information of the caterer because everything was delicious. While everyone was finishing up their entrée course, Governor Pearson took to the podium and began to speak.

"I hope everyone is having a great evening. I just wanted to take this opportunity to say a few words and thank everyone that has had a hand in making this year a great one for the state of Indiana. Without your support, I don't think that I could do my job successfully. I have a lot planned for the upcoming year to keep Indiana progressing forward and I know that we shouldn't have a problem getting it done. Would the planning committee please stand?" About five or six people stood up all around the room. "Look at these bright and shining faces here. These are the people responsible for putting this night together. They did an excellent job, don't you agree?" The committee looked around nervously as the crowd applauded in agreement.

"I'm not going to hold you guys too much longer because I've got chocolate molten lava cake waiting for me over there," he said and the room erupted with laughter. "But seriously, thank you guys. Thank you to everyone in this room. The state of Indiana is in great hands."

Everyone applauded as Governor Pearson walked back to his seat. The servers came back over to take our entrée plates and give us our dessert. Just as I was about to dig into my cheesecake, Taylor leaned over to whisper something to me. "Walk with me over to the bar when you're done with your dessert." I nodded my head in acknowledgement and continued to eat my cheesecake. The band had gotten back in their spots and started playing music. A few people who were already done with dessert had moved to the dance floor in the middle of the room and begun dancing. I finished my dessert and then leaned over to let Desmond know that I would be right back. Taylor and I walked over to the bar and ordered two Cosmopolitans. The bartender handed us our drinks and Taylor walked over to the corner of the room to an empty table while I followed. She took a sip of her drink before finally speaking.

"Have you given anymore thought to what we talked about in Miami?"

"Taylor, that was four months ago. What did we talk about in Miami?"

Taylor rolled her eyes and sucked her teeth. "Don't act like you don't remember. We talked about getting out of this life. Have you thought about it anymore?"

"No I haven't thought anymore about it. I see you every day. Why would you bring this up tonight?"

"The office really isn't the place to bring this up."

I waved my hand around to scan the room. "And bringing it up here is?"

"Look, I know my timing is bad but sitting there talking to those men at the table with us made me realize how much I don't want to do this anymore. I was hoping that you shared the same sentiment."

"The only thing that I agree with you on is that we don't want to do this forever. However, like I said before, getting out right now isn't a good idea. Let's set a date, make a plan and stick to it and then we can get out."

"Fallon," Taylor said and sighed heavily. "Can't you see that I am unhappy? I am miserable. Sometimes I can't even sleep at night because all I can think about is what would happen if we got caught. Why can't you see that?"

"That's probably because the only thing that I see is you spending money and living lavish. Don't act like you're not sitting up at night in a luxury apartment with 1200 thread count sheets. Let me ask you something; say we do give all us this up tomorrow...what are your plans? What are you going to do for work? Do you even have any money saved?"

"I don't know. I haven't thought that far down the line but I'm sure I'll figure it out. Whatever I do, I'm sure I'll be happier doing that than sitting here acting like we really belong in this room with these people."

I calmly put my drink down but inside I was fuming. "Well I tell you what. Call Goldie yourself and tell him that YOU want out. I'm sure I can manage just fine without you."

61

"You know what? I think I will!" Taylor slammed her drink down so hard that the bottom of the glass broke and the rest of the drink spilled and instantly stained the white tablecloth. She stormed off and walked back to our table. I watched as she leaned over and whispered something to Brent and he stood up and led her to the door. Desmond began walking over to me with a confused look on his face. I downed the rest of my drink before he got over to me. I would need it to finish this night.

"Is everything okay? What was that all about?"

"It was nothing. Girl stuff. Do you want to dance?"

"You know I want to dance. Don't be out here stepping on my feet. You know you can't dance."

"Boy please."

I took my dress in both hands and raised the bottom so my train wouldn't drag and led the way to the dance floor. The band had begun to play an instrumental version of Earth, Wind and Fire's 'September'. Desmond and I began to dance and play around on the dance floor. Even thought I was still a little upset with what just happened with Taylor, I could never stay mad for long with Desmond around. The band ended that song and began to play a slower song. Desmond took both of my hands and drew me in closer to him. I put my arms around his neck and laid my head on his chest. I felt like I could stay that way forever. All of a sudden, Desmond pulled back from me.

"I um…I have to um…I have to go to the bathroom. I'll be right back," he said and he quickly walked away before I could say anything. I stood there for a second dazed and confused until someone lightly tapped me on my shoulder. It was Mitch Walters.

"Well I was coming over here to ask your friend if it was okay for me to cut in but he ran off before I could. Would you like to dance?" He held out his hand. I smiled and took it and we began to sway to the beat.

"Don't you know my friend? Desmond Peters?"

"No. I don't think I've ever seen him before tonight."

I stopped dancing and just stared at him. "Wait…so he's not your social media director?"

"I don't think so. The last time I checked our social media directors' name is Chandler Ryan and he's right over there," he said as he pointed to a tall, blonde haired young white man with glasses that was taking pictures with his phone over by the Governor.

—

"Wow. That's interesting."

"Interesting indeed. I mean if he were interested in a position with the Pacers, I would definitely encourage him to apply. If he knows you then I'm sure he's good people."

I doubt it, I thought to myself. Between Taylor's blow up and Desmond obviously lying to me this entire time, my judge of character was a bit off.

"I wanted to come over here and thank you personally for your services. It is always quick, discreet and efficient. Not to mention the quality of the product is superb. I may need to double my order for next month."

"Thank you so much. Just let me know and I'll make it happen."

"I'm not sure if you were interested, but I have a little with me if you needed something to get you through the rest of this party," he said as he lightly tapped his tuxedo pocket.

I laughed. "No thank you sir. I just supply, I never participate."

"Understandable. Well I'll let you get back to your evening." He leaned over and gave me a peck on my cheek and then went back to join his wife at their table. I went to go find Desmond. I decided not to bring up that I knew he was lying about where he worked. I wanted to see if he would tell me himself. I really wanted to know why though. Did he do it just to try and impress me? It just seemed like such a silly thing to lie about. I found Desmond by the small bar outside near the lobby.

"There you are. Are you okay?"

"Yes I'm fine. I think it was that asparagus. I don't think it agreed with me too well," he said and grabbed his stomach.

"Do you want to leave? You've probably already stunk up the bathroom."

Desmond laughed at me. "Yeah let's get out of here. I'm sure the janitor walked in there and was instantly pissed."

We walked through the lobby and out to the entrance where everyone's limo or drivers were waiting. We spotted our limo and walked over to it. Desmond opened the door for me and slid in shortly after me. As the driver pulled off and began driving back to my apartment, Desmond put his arm around me and pulled me closer to him.

"Thank you for inviting me tonight. I had a great time."

"Thank you for coming. You looked slightly decent tonight."

—

63

Desmond smacked his lips. "Girl you know I look good. You see the governors' date was looking over at me like she wanted some of this chocolate to go with that cake."

I pretended to gag. "That's so gross."

"It's okay to be jealous. I only have eyes for you though."

We pulled up to my apartment and Desmond opened the door and let me out.

"Is it okay if I come up?"

"Not tonight. It's kind of late and I have a really busy day tomorrow. I'll call you in the morning."

"Okay that's cool. You get you some rest and don't forget to call me in the morning."

Desmond gave me a kiss on my forehead and then got back into the limo. I walked into the lobby and the other doorman had already relieved Archie for the night. I said hello and kept walking towards the elevator. I couldn't wait until I got upstairs to take this dress and these shoes off. I walked in my apartment and made a beeline to my bedroom. I hung up my fur stole in the closet and kicked off my shoes. I slipped my dress off and hung it next to the stole. I took off all of my jewelry and put them in their designated holders. I went to the bathroom and grabbed an Aveeno cleansing wipe and proceeded to wipe off all of my makeup and removed my lashes. I applied some moisturizer and then headed to my bed with just my panties and bra on. I grabbed my iPad off of my nightstand and went to Google. I went to the Pacers website and looked at all of the staff that they had pictured on their site. No Desmond Peters. I did see Chandler Ryan though. I went back to Google and typed in just Desmond Peters into the search bar. A lot of results came up but none of them were the right Desmond Peters. I typed in Rocky Peters. A number of results popped up about him playing football at Vanderbilt University but one link in particular caught my eye. I clicked on it and it was a news article from almost five years earlier. "Vanderbilt Running Back Indicted on Robbery Charges." I scanned through the article and it said that Daniel Peters, or Rocky, was indicted along with two other Vanderbilt students for robbing another student at gunpoint. According to the article, he wasn't even from Miami. He was from Baton Rouge, Louisiana. He had been kicked off of the football team and expelled from school. I stared at the mug shot in the article and sure enough, it was Desmond...or 'Daniel'. I typed Daniel Rocky Peters into the search bar. There were a number of articles about him for football but most were news articles about him being arrested for that robbery. I picked up my phone to call and curse him out but before I could press talk another headline caught my eye. "Murder Charges Dropped for Former Football Stand Out." I clicked on the article and noticed that my hands were shaking. I scanned through the article. Desmond had been charged with murder in Baton Rouge, Louisiana but was found not guilty due to a lack of evidence. I looked at the date on the article. The article was only a year old. I scrolled further through the article and was met by Desmond's mug shot. He had the nerve to be smiling. I shut off my iPad. I couldn't believe this. A criminal had finessed me. How could I have been so stupid? Just then my phone buzzed with a text. It was Desmond.

Thank you again for tonight. I had a ball. Sweet dreams Beautiful.
11:39 PM

I looked at the text and immediately felt nauseous. How could you sit here and be okay with lying to somebody you claimed to care about? I turned my phone off. I sat there for a minute watching TV but I couldn't even focus. I felt violated and I needed answers. I fell asleep trying to come up with a plan to get them.

The next morning I walked into the office and greeted Kayla and headed for Taylor's office. I softly knocked on the door. Taylor looked up from her computer and once she seen it was me, she rolled her eyes and went back to typing.
"Well good morning to you too Taylor. You can't possibly still be upset." Taylor continued to type.
"Wow, really? You're just going to give me the silent treatment?" Taylor continued to type. Her office phone began to ring. She let it ring until it stopped. It quickly began to ring again.
"Are you going to get that?" Taylor stopped typing to take a sip of her coffee and then went right back to her computer. I didn't have time for this.
"I guess. Have a great day Taylor."
I walked down to my office and immediately logged into my own computer. While it loaded, I quickly glanced over into Taylor's office. She was really about to sit here and have an attitude all day. Well I could have an attitude too. I definitely wasn't going to apologize to her because I don't think I did anything wrong. I logged

—
65

into my emails and began to check my inbox. There were a few inquiries that I left unread. I opened one email that instantly made my mouth drop. One of our clients, a famous restaurateur from New York, emailed us to say that he hadn't received his shipment for the month. I opened a new tab and logged into the payment system that we used to check his account. He had definitely made his payment for the month so I was very confused about why he hadn't received his product. I emailed him back and told him that I would look into finding out why he hadn't received his shipment on time and planned to send more than he ordered as an apology. I checked a few more emails and it was all clients saying the same thing; their shipments were either late or they hadn't received them at all this month. What was going on? Just then my office phone rang.

"This is Fallon Scott."

"Hey Fallon, this is Draya."

My heart dropped into the bottom of my stomach. Why on Earth would she be calling me? I quickly got myself together.

"Hey Draya! I haven't heard from you in a long time. What's going on?"

"Well I've been trying to call your partner all morning but apparently she's been ignoring my calls."

"Yes, she's been acting weird all morning. I don't know what's going on with her," I said, lying through my teeth. I knew exactly what was wrong with her.

"I'm assuming that you've checked your emails this morning."

"Yes I just did. Is there something wrong with the shipments? Pretty much all of our clients, minus a few are saying they haven't received their product this month. Do you know what's going on?"

"I don't but as you can imagine, Goldie isn't too pleased. He's actually requesting for you two to come down here."

"Really? When?"

"Tonight. He wants to meet with you all in the morning. You should be receiving your tickets here shortly."

As soon as she said that my computer chimed, notifying me of a new email. It was the plane tickets.

"Okay. I'll see you later on tonight."

Whatever was going on had to be serious because Goldie never requested to see us. As long as the money was right and everyone got paid on time, he usually left us alone. I got up and walked down to Taylor's office.

"Hey Taylor…Taylor…TAYLOR!"

Taylor spun around in her chair. "What? I obviously don't want to speak to you."

"Well get over it and check your email. We have to go and see Goldie."

Chapter 6

It's something about being in Houston that automatically brings a sense of calm over me. You would think that after being away for so many years it would feel like a foreign place but as soon as I stepped off of the plane and into the brisk southern air, I instantly felt right back at home. Taylor and I had some of our highest highs and bottom of the earth's core lows here. Unfortunately this wasn't a vacation or trip for pleasure. As long as we had been doing this we had never had a problem with our shipments, payments or pleasing our customers but in this business, if the money is messed up, the entire operation is messed up. Both Taylor and I were uneasy about meeting with Goldie because we honestly had no answers for him. Our plane had landed and instead of us ordering a car, Draya insisted that we let Tone come and pick us up. We waited at the cellphone lot for him but he still hadn't arrived. We decided to go back into the airport and grab a drink while we waited. Since we had some free time I pulled out the manila folder I had in my carry on and began looking over the paperwork for our shipments and client orders. Taylor followed suit and pulled out her paperwork from her bag. Ever since Draya called us I had been reviewing all of our files just to see if I had missed anything important or if anything looked out of the ordinary. I didn't find anything wrong. The only conclusion that I could come up with is that there was an issue on Goldie's end. Taylor handled all of the money that came in and she was just as stressed as I was because she literally broke a sweat reviewing the books from this month.

"Are you okay Thing 2?"

Taylor wiped her forehead with the small napkin that had come with her drink she'd ordered.

"Yes I'm fine. I just don't understand this. I keep checking and double-checking the books and everything is fine. The issue isn't us."

"I don't see an issue with my paperwork either. I don't know what the problem is. Maybe Goldie has it figured out."

"Yeah I hope you're right," she said as she picked up her drink and downed the rest of it. She signaled the bartender and ordered another one.

"You better slow down Taylor. You need to be on your A game when we get to Goldie."

"I'm not going to get sloppy. I just need to calm my nerves."

Before I could respond my phone buzzed with a text from Tone letting us know he had just pulled up.

"Come on. Tone is outside."

We gathered our luggage and walked back to the cellphone lot. When we got outside Tone flashed the headlights of the black Suburban he was driving to get our attention. We walked over to the truck and began to load our luggage into the back seat. Taylor hopped into the front seat while I slid into the back with our bags.

"What's up ladies? How was your flight?"

"Hey Tone, our flight was okay. I missed you. I haven't seen you in forever," I said as I wrapped my arms around his neck from behind the headrest.

"I missed you too. Ya'll need to start coming back down here and visiting more often. I guess you're just going to sit there acting brand new?" Tone playfully shoved Taylor and we all laughed.

"I'm not acting brand new. You know I missed you too Tone. I'm just a little tired."

"Well we'll be at Goldie's soon. Are you ladies hungry?"

"Yes, we're starving. We can just stop and get something quick. We don't have to sit down."

Tone nodded his head and continued to work his way through the busy traffic near the airport. I was so consumed with the paperwork and Taylor was so busy looking at her phone that we didn't notice when Tone had pulled up to the drive thru window at Whataburger. We placed our orders and once we received our food, Tone got back on the highway and we headed to Goldie's estate. Goldie lived in the River Oaks section of Houston in an enormous 5 bedroom, 8-bathroom house. As we carefully maneuvered through the winding road and up the hill to the house, I couldn't help but stare in awe at all of the other huge multimillion-dollar homes in the area out of the window. *One day I'll have one of these of my own*, I said to myself. We pulled up in the circular driveway and Tone said, "You guys go ahead and go in. I'm going to park the truck."

We gathered our luggage from the back and got out of the truck. We walked up to the side door of the tan brick home and knocked on the door. A few moments later the light above the door flashed on and then quickly flashed off and we could see the blinds moving. The door swung open shortly after and Draya stood there in a sheer black robe exposing her naked body, beaming at us.

"Hey ladies! I'm so glad to see you guys. Come on in. I'll show you where you can put your things"

She reached over and gave both of us hugs. I tried not to blush as her bare breasts brushed against me. Taylor and I stepped into the house and followed as Draya led us through the kitchen. She still looked exactly like the first time that we met her except for she had grown her sandy brown hair out and it swung from side to side down her back as she walked. The entire house had a very rustic feel with high ceilings and exposed wood beams. The kitchen had tan wood cabinets, brown granite counter tops and a small chandelier hanging above the large island. We passed the dining room and walked up the black winding staircase until we made it to the third story of the home. There were three spare bedrooms and two bathrooms on that level and after peeking into each room, Taylor and I decided on a room and went to put our bags down. The room that I chose had a gray queen sized platform bed and black dressers and nightstands. The adjoining bathroom had the same brown granite countertops like the kitchen and a standalone shower with a detachable showerhead inside. After I put my things down, I went down the hall to see the room that Taylor picked. Her room had the same style platform bed that mine had but the headboard was blue. Her dressers and nightstands were cherry oak and her bathroom was identical to mine. Draya was standing in front of the full-length mirror in Taylor's room retying her robe.

"Are you ladies hungry? I know you're probably tired after your flight."

I shook my head. "No, Tone stopped at Whataburger for us. I don't know about Taylor but I'm exhausted. We had a really long day." Taylor nodded in agreement. "I'm worn out too. Draya where is Goldie?"

"He's downstairs in the living room. If you ladies are ready we can go ahead and go down there."

We followed Draya out of the room and down the stairs to the living room. Before we turned the corner to enter the room we could hear the sound of someone playing a piano. We entered the room and seen that it was actually Goldie that was playing. The living room had all white plush furniture with gold accents throughout the room. There was a stone fireplace that wasn't lit, but it was clearly the focal point of the room. In the right corner there were large floor to ceiling windows that gave us a direct view of the pool in the backyard. The white baby grand piano sat in that corner as well and once we stepped all the way into the room, we could see Goldie. He was so focused on playing the piano that he didn't even notice that we had walked in. Goldie looked exactly the same as the first time I had seen him; he still had the neatly maintained curly hair and the goatee but from where I was standing I could see a few gray curls that were taking over his temples. Draya walked over and put her arms around his neck from behind and leaned down and whispered something in his ear. Goldie looked up and over into the direction where Taylor and I were standing. His lips slowly curved into a smile and he slid off of the piano bench and began walking over to us. He had on a black smoking robe, black pants and leather house slippers. As he made it over to us he stopped in front of me and extended his arms for a hug.

"Well if it isn't Thing 1 and Thing 2. You ladies look great."

I returned his hug and he stepped over to Taylor to give her one too.

"You look good too Goldie. I didn't know you knew how to play the piano."

"Well I'm a man of many talents," he said and brushed the shoulders of his robe off. We all laughed. "Are you ladies hungry? We still have leftovers from dinner in there if you want them."

"No thank you. Tone stopped and got us something to eat. Draya you cooked dinner?"

Draya scoffed and looked at me like I was crazy. "Now you know I'm not cooking anything. We have a chef that comes and does all the dirty work for me."

Goldie grabbed her hand and pulled her close to him. "It's okay baby. You know I didn't marry you for your cooking anyway."

Draya smiled and leaned in and began to kiss him. Taylor and I both looked at each other with disgusted looks on our faces. Standing

—

71

there while they continued to kiss was extremely awkward so I decided to break the tension.

"I don't mean to interrupt but Goldie we're both a little tired. Are we meeting tonight?"

"Oh no, I figured you all would want to rest so we're going to meet first thing in the morning. You all go ahead and get you some rest." We both gave Goldie another hug and then headed back upstairs to our rooms.

"How awkward was that?" Taylor whispered as we walked up the steps.

"I know right? I knew I had to interrupt them. All I could see was those robes coming off in my head and I didn't want to see that at all."

We both laughed. Taylor walked into her room, telling me goodnight before she softly closed the door.

I laid across the bed and looked for an electrical outlet on the wall. There was one right behind the nightstand. I grabbed my purse and took the phone charger that I kept in there out and unraveled it as I plugged it into the wall. I grabbed my phone out of my purse and pressed the home button to see that my phone was on 7%. I quickly attached it to the charger and made sure to take it off of airplane mode. As soon as I did that my phone began to chime with missed texts and calls. They were all from Desmond. I wasn't ready to talk to him just yet. I was trying to figure out how to confront him about him lying to me but I hadn't found the right words to say so I decided to just ignore him for the time being. I read all of his messages and listened to all of his voicemails. They were all him asking if I was okay and for me to call him. He seemed genuinely concerned but I still wasn't ready to talk to him. I set the alarm on my phone for 7 and then rolled over and shut my eyes. I don't think I even lasted ten minutes before I fell into a deep sleep.

The next morning my phone buzzed and rung out with the annoying noise that I had it programmed to. I immediately pressed the snooze button. I needed at least another hour of sleep to be able to function for the rest of the day. When my alarm rang for the second time, Taylor walked into the room and plopped down on the bed, already dressed for the day.

"Wake up Thing 1. Goldie and Draya are already downstairs eating breakfast."

I sat up in the bed and began to stretch. "Man…I wish we could sleep in today. That plane ride has me drained."

"Me too. I'll probably take a nap after this meeting is over."

"I'm going to take a shower and get dressed. Do you want to stay in here or are you going to go ahead and go get something to eat?" Taylor cocked her head and furrowed her brow. "Now you know I'm not going down there by myself. I'm just going to sit here until you get ready."

I laughed and began to get my clothes ready. I opted to copy Taylor's wardrobe choice for the day: jeans, a fitted t-shirt and my Giuseppe sneakers. I went to the bathroom and took a quick shower and brushed my teeth. My hair was still intact from my salon visit the week before so I applied a little makeup and then walked back to the room and grabbed my phone.

"Your phone has been buzzing nonstop while you were in the shower."

I pressed the home button. There were more texts from Desmond. I rolled my eyes. "It's just Desmond. Nobody important."

"Nobody important? Are you and Desmond about to call it quits or something?"

"I think so. I'll tell you all about it after this meeting. Let's go ahead and head downstairs before Goldie sends Draya up here for us."

I grabbed the manila folder from my carry on and began walking down the hall towards the steps.

"Wait a second. I have to get my paperwork out of my room." I waited at the top of the stairs for Taylor to come back from her room. When she did, we walked down the steps and were immediately greeted by the smell of bacon. As soon as I smelled the food, my stomach began to growl. Draya and Goldie were already at the table eating while Tone and another guy were sitting on the bar stools in front of the island eating. There were platters of food lined along the counter; there were pancakes, waffles, bacon, sausage links, scrambled eggs, grits and fresh fruit. A man with a white chef's jacket and hat was at the sink washing dishes.

"Good morning sleepy heads. I thought you all weren't going to come down until lunch time." Goldie greeted us and everyone's head turned in our direction.

I smiled. "Oh Goldie, its only 8:30. You didn't have to hire a chef and cook all of this food just for us."

73

Everybody except for Taylor and me began to laugh. Taylor and I looked at each other, both confused.

"This isn't just for you; this is how we eat every day. Here, come and meet my chef. Ladies, this is Chef Warren. Warren, this is Taylor and Fallon. They're like daughters to me."

Chef Warren grabbed a dishtowel and dried his hands before extending them to shake ours. "It's a pleasure to meet you all. I hope you both enjoy the food as long as you're here."

"Come over here ladies, there's someone else I want you to meet." Goldie led us over to the barstools where Tone and the other man were sitting. The other man got off of his tool and stood up. He had to be at least 6'4. He was solid, with muscles bulging out of his shirt, completely opposite of Tone who was also tall but he was essentially a big teddy bear. He was caramel brown skinned with a low haircut and dark eyes. I noticed a scar on his neck that went from his earlobe to the top of his collarbone. Seeing that immediately sent chills down my spine. Taylor tapped me on my leg and we shared a familiar look with one another. We both agreed that he was gorgeous.

"Taylor, Fallon…this is Bentley. He is working security for me with Tone."

Bentley extended his hand out to us. "It's nice to meet you ladies. I've heard a lot about you." Both Taylor and I shared another look, this time it was one of surprise. Bentley's voice was very deep and gritty. It didn't match his appearance at all. We both shook his hand and smiled back.

"It's nice to meet you as well. You definitely make us feel secure." Everyone began to laugh. I set the folder down on the table and made my way over to the counter where the food was waiting. Taylor set her folder down on the island and sat on the stool right next to Bentley.

"Is it okay if I sit here?"

Bentley smiled at her and nodded his head. I chuckled to myself. Taylor wasted no time letting it be known that she wanted him. I fixed my plate and then went back to the table. Chef Warren brought me a champagne flute filled with a Mimosa and then walked back over to finish fixing Taylor's. I observed the room while I ate. Goldie was at the head of the table reading the newspaper, Draya wasn't really eating but she was on her second Mimosa since we'd been downstairs. Tone and Bentley were laughing and joking around while Taylor tried to include herself in the conversation. Chef

—

74

Warren had finished washing the dishes and had begun chopping up vegetables for whatever he was making for lunch. From the outside looking in you would never think that the room was filled with drug dealers and trained killers but that's exactly what we were. I wondered if Chef Warren knew how Goldie was so wealthy or if he even cared. I finished my food and took my plate over to the sink. Chef Warren looked at me and smiled.

"Are you sure you don't want seconds? There's more than enough left over."

"No thank you. I'm stuffed. Everything was great though. Thank you so much."

"My pleasure. If you loved breakfast, you're going to love lunch. I hope you like pasta."

Taylor walked over and put her plate into the sink. Goldie looked up from his newspaper.

"Well since you ladies are finished we can go ahead and head to my office. Grab your paperwork."

We grabbed the folders and followed Goldie as he walked down the hall to his office. There was an enormous mahogany desk in the center of the room along with a burgundy leather chair behind it and two smaller chairs in front of it. There was a black leather couch on the right side of the room along with a TV and a treadmill. The left side of the room was nothing but a built in bookshelf that took up the entire wall and was filled with books. Goldie walked over to the burgundy chair.

"You ladies go ahead and have a seat."

We nervously sat down and waited for Goldie to continue. Goldie turned on the screen of his computer and waited a couple of seconds before typing something into the keyboard.

"First of all let me say that you ladies have done an amazing job with the consulting business. I was a little nervous at first when I chose you, but you both have exceeded my expectations."

We both smiled. That calmed our nerves a little and we began to relax.

"So yesterday I was notified by our delivery men that they haven't received payment and since they haven't been paid, they haven't delivered any shipments this month. Any idea what happened to their payment?"

"That's impossible Goldie. Both Taylor and I have checked our documents multiple times and there's nothing wrong on our end. We

---

have an efficient system in place that makes everything run smoothly."

"Explain that process to me, if you don't mind."

"Sure. Let's pretend that you're a new customer. I do all of the onboarding for us, which includes taking all of your information and putting it into our system. I then take your payment information and create a bit coin wallet for you. After the account is created, they receive their login information for our online store. There they can make their orders and pick how much or how little product they need. If they have a set amount of product that they want every month, for instance if you wanted to purchase five kilos every month, we will send you an invoice at the end of every month and you can pay using your bit coin wallet that way. After we've received their payments, we send them a tracking number for their shipment and their package is delivered to a secure location that the customer has chosen."

"And you're still using the delivery company that I told you to? You haven't begun using or paying another company?"

"Yes. We haven't changed anything."

"Interesting," he said as he leaned back in the chair and began twirling his goatee in between his fingers. "And Taylor, you have a system in place for distributing funds?"

Taylor nodded. "Yes I do. All customers receive their invoices on the 25th of the month. If their invoice isn't paid by the 30th or 31st, we discontinue their services and dissolve their bit coin wallet."

"What about your payments to the delivery company? How often do you pay them?"

"They send us an invoice every month and we pay them as soon as we received it through our automated system."

"Do they give you a receipt?"

"They do. You should be able to see every invoice from the delivery company and all of the bills from our office including our receptionist Kayla's salary on your end."

"That's right. I should." Goldie shifted his chair and began typing. He stopped typing and began reading the screen while he sat back in the chair and twirled his goatee. Both Taylor and I sat there nervously but we didn't dare move or say anything to interrupt him. Goldie finally stopped reading and clapped his hands together, startling the both of us.

—

"Alright ladies, everything looks good on our end. I'll have to take this up with the delivery company and see what's going on so we can get this cleared up with them. I've already gotten our customers taken care of so you shouldn't have to worry about them. I have you all leaving Sunday morning so I guess you all can go and enjoy the weekend. I'm sure there's some people from college here that you all want to meet up with."

Taylor and I slowly got up and began walking to the door.

"Oh…and before you leave, let me get those folders from you. We can't leave information like that lying around."

I walked over and set my manila folder on his desk. Taylor was still standing in the same spot.

"Is there something wrong Taylor?"

Taylor looked nervous but quickly shook her head no. "There's nothing wrong but why do you need our information if you can see everything from your computer?"

Goldie sat there for a few moments staring at Taylor and then slowly began to smile.

"You know what, you're right. You can go ahead and keep yours. You ladies enjoy your day."

We turned around and walked up the steps to our rooms in silence. I couldn't believe Taylor said that to Goldie. Why make a big deal about him asking for the folder if all of the information was right on both ends? And if it weren't wouldn't he have said something in the meeting? We both separated and walked into our rooms. I laid across the bed and closed my eyes for a nap. I did want to stop by the Galleria at some point but I needed just a couple of minutes of sleep so that I wouldn't burn out completely. Just as I began to drift off, my phone buzzed with a text message. I grabbed my phone and rolled my eyes, expecting for it to be Desmond. It was Goldie.

Draya is going to come upstairs and ask you to go shopping with her and Taylor. Turn her down. I need to talk to you while they're gone.
10:02 AM

I stared at my screen, extremely confused. What could he possibly have to talk to me about? Like clockwork, there was a soft knock at my door. Draya cracked the door a little, seen that I was awake and slowly opened it all the way and came inside.

"Hey girl. I'm thinking about going to the mall in a few. Did you want to come?"

Remembering what Goldie's message said, I shook my head no. "No thank you. I need to take a nap. I'm still trying to catch up on sleep from our flight."

"Alright I'll let you slide this time but you're not off the hook. We're going out later on tonight and you ARE going so don't try to get out of it."

"I promise I won't. Bring me back a pretzel or something."

Draya scrunched her face up and tilted her head back. "The only thing I'm bringing back is clothes and shoes. You better come with us if you want a pretzel."

"I guess I'll just miss out this time. Have fun!"

Draya walked out and began to close the door. "Oh you can leave it open."

I heard Draya walk down the hall and ask Taylor if she was ready. I heard the both of them talking and giggling as they walked down the steps. I waited 20 minutes or so before I got up just to make sure they were really gone. Once I assumed the coast was clear, I got up and headed downstairs to Goldie's office. I softly knocked on the door and Goldie was sitting behind his desk while Tone and Bentley sat in the chairs in front of him. Once they seen me standing there they immediately got up and began standing on either side of Goldie. "Come on in Fallon. Have a seat."

I cautiously walked in and slowly sat down in front of him. "What's going on Goldie?"

"I wanted to speak to you by yourself because I have some concerns about your partner that I wanted to bring to your attention."

"What kind of concerns?"

"Well first let me ask this; Fallon would you say that you trusted Taylor?"

"Of course I trust her. That's my best friend. Is there a reason why I shouldn't?"

Goldie smiled at me and then got up from the desk and walked over to my chair.

"Fallon go sit in my seat."

What was going on? I got up and walked over to the large leather chair and sat down. The computer screen was unlocked and still had the records from all of our transactions up. Goldie walked over to the bookcase and began to thumb through the different books, stopping on one and pulling it out, flipping through the pages and then putting it back. He did this three more times before finally speaking.

"Has Taylor ever given you any reason not to trust her with the money?"

"No. You know that's her lane. She's good with numbers so I just let her do her thing and she lets me do mine."

"Has she been unhappy or said anything about being displeased with the job?"

"Well," I hesitated. I didn't want to say anything wrong but Goldie could always tell when I wasn't telling the whole truth. "She had been talking to me about wanting to get out of the business and going legit."

"And what did you say to that?"

"I told her that now wasn't a good time and we should wait a couple of years to save up some money."

"That sounds like a good plan," he said as he walked back over to the desk and sat in one of the chairs at the front. "What did she say when you told her to wait?"

I wiped my hands on my pants. My palms had begun to sweat and Tone and Bentley standing beside me didn't make me feel any better. "Well she wasn't happy about it. She kept saying how she didn't want to wait and she wanted out now."

"That's interesting. Fallon do me a favor. Read those documents on the screen and let me know when you're done."

I wiggled the computer mouse because the screen had gone into sleep mode and began reading the documents. There was a side by side of Goldie's system and Taylor's system. There were a lot of numbers but you could clearly see where the numbers that we received were different from the numbers that Taylor had reported that we took in. At first they were only different by a couple of dollars but as I continued to scroll the difference in numbers began to get bigger. I glanced at Goldie and he was staring at me with a smirk on his face.

"Do you understand what you're reading?"

I nodded. "Taylor has been stealing?"

Goldie nodded back. "Scroll down to August. That was when you all signed the deal with the governor."

I scrolled down and read the screen and my mouth immediately dropped. After Governor Pearson signed with us, our intake for that week alone was supposed to be $4.2 million dollars. Taylor had only reported $40,000. I stared at the computer screen in disbelief. I scrolled down some more and looked at the following months and Taylor continued to report the numbers wrong. Because she had reported them wrong, it put us in the red and completely drained our company account. We didn't have enough available funds to make the payment to the delivery company. We were barely able to pay Kayla this month. Why would she do this? She could get us both killed. It wasn't until Tone had tapped me on my shoulder and handed me a tissue that I noticed that I was crying.

"Goldie I swear to you, I had no idea that this was going on."

"I believe you. You know Fallon; we've always had our own relationship separate from Taylor. I saw something in you that first night that we met that always stuck with me. You've proved to be trustworthy and loyal. Taylor on the other hand has never been a big fan of me. Trust me, the feeling is mutual. When we set the back end of this business up I always had my doubts about her so I had my other computer tech give me access to her side of the business. No offense."

"None taken. You obviously had the right idea."

"I've been watching her the entire time you all have been in business and for the first five years she did everything right. But this year, for whatever reason, she has been robbing us blind."

"So what is going to happen now? What are you going to do to her?" Goldie looked at Tone and Bentley and they began to laugh. "Why, I'm going to kill her of course."

"Goldie, no. Please don't hurt her. Let me figure something out." Goldie stared at me and smirked. "Fallon are you into gardening?" I stared at him blankly. "Goldie, I live on the 25th floor of a high rise. I know nothing about gardening."

All three of the men began to laugh. I was dead serious and didn't find anything funny.

"Well Fallon, you may not know a lot about gardening but do you know why we have to pull the weeds when gardening?"

"Because they'll end up ruining the garden?"

"Exactly. Weeds rob your soil and everything that you worked hard to plant of the nutrients and water that they need. I'd like to think of Taylor as our weed that we need to pull. She's already been robbing us for an entire year. Before I see this business crumble and fail because of her, she has to go."

"Goldie," I leaned forward on the desk and put my head in my hands and began to rub my temples. "Please don't hurt her. I know she messed up big time. But give me some time to come up with a plan to get her away from the business. There has to be another way for us to go about this."

Goldie stood up and began to slowly pace in front of the desk. "Tone, Bentley...what do you all think?"

Tone clasped his hands together and began cracking his knuckles. "You know how I feel boss. She's got to go. I don't care how we do it or if she's even breathing when it's all over. A thief is the worst thing you can be."

"I agree, I agree. What about you Bentley?"

"I see what you're saying sir and you know it doesn't make a difference to me one way or another but if Fallon feels like she can come up with a way for us to get rid of her without any bloodshed then I think we should hear her out."

Goldie continued to pace until finally he stopped and sat back down. "Okay Fallon. If you can figure out how to get rid of her without us having to get our hands dirty, then make it happen. But you do have a deadline. She has to be gone by the end of the month. I'm not starting the New Year with her continuing to steal from us. I hope you know that I'm only letting this slide as a favor to you."

"Thank you so much Goldie," I said as I hopped up from the chair and walked around the desk to give him a hug. "I'm going to figure this out. I promise you won't have to worry about her anymore. Am I free to go?"

"Yes you can go ahead and go. Let me know what you come up with later."

I slowly walked out of the room. I could feel all three of their eyes burning through my back and I could tell that they were waiting for me to be out of earshot before they started to speak. When I got outside of the door I sat there for a second and just listened.

"That was awfully noble of you, boss. You usually never let anything like that slide."

"I know. Fallon is lucky I love her. I don't know what kind of hold Taylor has on her but I should've killed that bitch a long time ago."

I couldn't listen anymore. I walked back up the steps and went to my room. I sat down on my bed and immediately put my head in my hands and began to cry. Goldie was right; Taylor did have a hold on me. Maybe it was the fact that she really was like a sister to me or perhaps it was because she looked out for me when we first met with my housing situation. In a way, I guess I always felt indebted to her. I got up off of the bed and walked to the bathroom. I grabbed a washcloth and wet it and began to wipe my face. I got myself together and reapplied my makeup. I didn't want Taylor and Draya to see my face all splotchy and swollen from crying once they got back. I went back over to the bed and grabbed my phone. Sometimes my slick talking got me in trouble because I sat up here and told Goldie that I would come up with a plan and I didn't even know where to start. I went to my contacts and scrolled through them looking for someone, anyone that could possibly help me out. I stopped scrolling at a familiar name and instantly began to smile. I pressed talk on the phone and listened to the phone ring as I stood up and nervously paced in front of the bed. Part of me was hoping that the call went to voicemail. They picked up.

"Hello?"

"Hey…this is Fallon. I'm in Houston for a couple of days and I was wondering if you wanted to do lunch?"

~~~

The line inside of Frank's Pizza was almost out of the door with people waiting for their individual slices and whole pies. I was already regretting my decision to come to a pizza place for lunch but this place was special to me. There were a lot of memories here and not to mention, the pizza was amazing. I sat there scrolling through my phone to pass time when a familiar voice stopped me in my tracks.

"Perhaps we should've called ahead to beat the lunch rush?"

I turned around in my seat and instantly began smiling. I stood up and wrapped my arms around Xavier's neck as he pulled me in for a hug. I had to stop myself from completely melting into his body but I kept my composure.

"It's so good to see you. It's been a long time."

"I know. I'm glad you called me. You need to come and visit Houston more often."

We sat down at the table and continued to wait on our pizza. Ever since we met we would always come down here and get a large chicken fiesta pizza. We had been here so much in the past that when I came in to put our order in, the men behind the counter said, "Hey!

—

82

Long time no see!" We both looked at each other nervously. Xavier still looked great. He had cut his braids off and he had gotten his braces removed. His suit was perfectly tailored to fit his body. We sat in awkward silence for a while, both of us not knowing what to say to one another. Just in the nick of time, the man behind the counter called our order number and set our pizza on the counter. "I'll go get it." Xavier walked over to the counter and picked up our pizza and cups. He placed the pizza on the table and then headed over to the drink machines to fill our cups. He pointed at the sweet tea dispenser and I nodded my head yes. He filled his cup with Pepsi, grabbed a stack of napkins and then headed back to the table. He set everything down and then grabbed both of my hands and we both put our heads down as he blessed the food. After we said amen, we both dug into the pizza.

"I've got to admit Fallon, I was a little surprised to see your name pop up on my screen today. No complaints of course, I just was a little shocked."

"Yes I know I contacted you out of the blue. I just knew I couldn't come down to Houston without at least giving you a call."

"Well I'm glad you thought about me. How's life treating you in Indy?"

"Life is okay. All I do is work and go home. How is life going for you Mr. Assistant District Attorney?"

"See that's why you need to keep in touch. I've been promoted. I am the *chief* assistant district attorney now."

I grabbed a napkin and wiped my mouth and hands off before beginning a small round of applause. "Look at you making big moves! You're getting closer and closer to that district attorney spot."

"Thank you, thank you. Yes, it seems like it's a long way off but I'm not stopping until I get the title. Business seems to be going good for you though," he said as he began playing with the diamond bangles on my wrist.

I smiled while slowly pulling my hand back from the table. "Business is pretty good; I can't complain. It could always be better though."

Xavier shook his head and smiled. "I'm sure it could. How's Taylor been?"

I'm sure my face gave away how I truly felt but I kept my composure and tried to play it off. "She's great. We've been busy so all she does is work too."

Xavier grabbed my hand. "Now Fallon, I think I know you better than anyone. Your face doesn't say that she's great. What's going on with you too?"

"Xavier," I paused for a moment. I needed to get my words together before responding. He didn't need to know all of the details. "How would you deal with knowing you need to end a business relationship without it affecting the personal relationship?"

"Well, you know I'm not a big fan of your business…"

"Trust me, I know." We both laughed. When I told Xavier about wanting to start the business, Xavier heavily objected. He assumed this 'job' that I had was just something to do while I was in school and that I would stop once I graduated. He had never known about Goldie specifically but he knew that the drugs weren't just appearing out of thin air. We argued for weeks and when the time came for me to graduate, Xavier hit me with an ultimatum; either I could have the business or I could have him but I couldn't have both. Looking back on it now, especially with Taylor screwing everything up, I think I made the wrong decision.

"I'm not a fan of the business but if I remember correctly, you all set everything up to look legit. If that is the case then you can simply buy her out of the partnership. I personally wouldn't be able to help you with that paperwork because I practice criminal law but I have some friends from law school that can definitely help you out."

"Really? Thank you so much! I'm willing to pay whatever I need to get this over with."

"She must've really done something terrible for you to be thinking about buying her out. You two used to be thick as thieves."

"Yeah well…let's just say she took the word thief a little too literally."

"Ahhh, okay. I think you'll be okay. I've seen you guys through some really rough times. I'm sure you all can be friends after this. Some people just can't be in business together."

I finished the last few bites of my pizza before I placed my napkin on the top of my plate and pushed it away. "Whew, I am stuffed. I'm sure I just gained another pound or two."

—

Xavier smiled and leaned over the side of the table to get a good view of my hips in the chair. "Well I'm sure those pounds are going to all of the right places."

"Here you go," I said while I blushed.

"Do you mind if I ask you something a bit personal?"

I shook my head no. "You know you can ask me anything. What's up?"

"You claim to be all work and no play but this weekend is like a vacation for you, right?"

"Well I guess you could say that. I got all of my work done earlier today."

"So how about you spend the rest of the weekend with me? I know you don't want to be cooped up in that hotel for the rest of your time here."

Sticking with the lie that I'd told him about me staying in a hotel, I nodded yes. "You're right; I don't want to stay there the entire weekend. I don't want to invade you or your girlfriend's space though *Smoke*." I winked after I said it.

"Ha-ha, very funny. That name disappeared as soon as I walked across the stage at graduation. You know I'm out here lonely. I should ask the same about you. I won't have any men knocking my door down because you're over there will I?"

I laughed. "Nope, I'm single. I told you all I do is work and go home. I'm boring." I didn't really think I was lying about that. I had already decided that it was over between me and Desmond, or whatever his name was.

"Okay so...let's be boring together this weekend."

"I'm down. Let me go and get my stuff from the hotel and then I guess I'll just meet you at your house once you get off."

"I tell you what," Xavier said while grabbing his keys from his pocket and then removing one of the keys from the ring. "Go get your stuff and then just head to my house. Here's the key and..." he grabbed a pen from his suit jacket pocket. He scribbled something down on a napkin before folding it and handing it to me. "...Here's the address."

I folded the napkin again and placed it inside of my purse. We both got up from the table and began to walk to the door. I had taken one of Goldie's cars to come and meet with Xavier so I began to walk towards where I parked. Xavier's office was located in the opposite direction of where I parked so before we parted ways, I extended my arms to him for a hug. He scooped me up and we stood there for a few minutes just taking in the moment. Xavier released the hug first and took a few seconds to gaze into my eyes. He took his hand and placed it under my chin and gently guided my face towards his.

When our lips met, I immediately felt like I was that 18-year-old girl again. When we finally came up for air, we both just stood there and smiled.

"Alright Xavier, I've got to go. I'll be waiting for you when you get home."

"Okay."

We both began to walk away. I knew that if I turned around I would see him staring. I had made it to the corner and was about to cross to get to the parking lot when I heard my name.

"Hey Fallon!"

I turned around and Xavier was still standing there. "Yes?"

He smiled at me. "I'm really, really glad that you called me today."

I smiled back at him. "I'm really, really glad that you answered."

Chapter 7

"Fallon are you okay? That's your third cup of coffee this morning. You usually never even touch the coffee."

I finished adding more creamer to my cup and then turned towards Kayla's desk.

"Yes I'm fine Kayla. I guess I'm still trying to get back into the routine after Houston."

"Yeah I understand. How was the trip?"

"It was okay. It's always good to go back to our old stomping grounds."

"I wish I could've gone to an out of state school. My parents were a little strict so the furthest I could go was to Purdue."

"Yeah well, parents mean well. Be glad that you have parents to be strict. I'm going to go ahead and head back to my office."

I walked back down the hall to my office, cautiously sipping the piping hot coffee along the way. As I passed Taylor's office, her head popped up from typing and she called out to me.

"Thing 1 did you still want to meet this morning? Or did you want to wait until after lunch?"

"Um…we can meet right now. Let me go to my office and get my paperwork and I'll be right back."

"Okay."

I continued walking back to my office. I was a nervous wreck. I had text Taylor the night before to let her know that I wanted to have a word with her when we got to work. I wasn't ready but this talk was necessary and the entire future of the company depended on it. When I got to my office I walked behind my desk and jiggled my mouse to get my computer screen to open. I went to my email inbox and

—

scrolled down to the email from the lawyer that Xavier had referred me to. I clicked on the files attached to the email and pressed print. I grabbed an empty manila folder from the drawer in my desk and gathered the paperwork. I went back over to my desk and gulped down the rest of my coffee, popped a few mints that I kept on my desk into my mouth, reapplied another layer of lip gloss and headed back to Taylor's office. When I walked back into her office she had been talking on her cellphone but immediately hung up once she seen me walk in, which I thought was odd. She hadn't even told the person she was talking to that she was hanging up.

"You didn't have to end your call. I could've waited until you finished."

"It's cool. The conversation was over anyway. So what's going on?" I sat there for a second and took a deep breath before I began to speak. "Well Taylor…you know you are my best friend, my sister and pretty much the only family that I have. We have been through so much together and I love you so much."

"I love you too Fallon. You called a meeting just to tell me that?" Taylor laughed nervously.

"Not exactly. We had been talking previously about how unhappy you've been in this business and how you've wanted to get out of it and live your life. I've heard you and I stand by my stance of wanting to wait a few years before completely getting out, but it's because I love you that I've come up with a solution that will be in the best interests of both of us. I've consulted with a lawyer who evaluated the value of the company and I've drafted up an agreement to buy you out of our partnership." I put the manila folder on Taylor's desk and gently pushed it towards her. Taylor picked the folder up and began to read the paperwork. I studied her face as she read but she kept a blank stare the entire time. Once she got to the last page of the agreement she closed the folder and set it back on the desk. She stared me directly in the eye and said, "Are you fucking kidding me?"

I furrowed my brow in confusion. "What's the problem Taylor?" Taylor sat there for a few seconds giving me the evil eye before finally speaking. "You are really that selfish that you would kick me out of the business?"

"Taylor, I'm not kicking you out of anything. You've said that you wanted out and I've come up with a way for you to do so. And it's not like I'm just leaving you with nothing. I'm paying you a pretty

—

decent amount of money. You have enough to completely start over if you wanted to."

"This 'decent amount of money' is a slap in my face. When I talked about getting out of this, I talked about US getting out. We were dragged into this together and I wanted us to get out together. We're a team! And I know how much this company is worth. I keep the books remember? This little agreement doesn't even begin to pay me what I'm worth."

"Well actually, the agreement was drafted based on the money that you've already stolen. If you add that amount to what I'm offering you, you'll see that you're getting more than your fair share."

Taylor's eyes got big. "What are you talking about Fallon?"

"Oh don't play coy with me Taylor. I've seen the finance reports and you've been stealing money all year. Goldie showed me."

"Goldie? Goldie put you up to this? I should've known that he had something to do with you wanting to get rid of me. He's always had it out for me."

I shook my head. "Now is not the time to play victim. I'm giving you an out, Taylor. I suggest you take it."

"I'm not taking anything. If I'm leaving, then you're leaving too. I can shut all of this down with the press of a button and nobody will leave with anything. I can't believe you Fallon. Here I was sitting here thinking that we were in this together and you've been all about yourself this entire time."

I was beginning to get irritated. I could feel my face begin to get hot. "I'm all about myself? Don't try to flip this around on me. You've been stealing from the company but I'm out for self? You're delusional."

"I only took that money to get back at Goldie. It had nothing to do with you. We sit here working hard and risking our lives making all of this money for him through the years and what do we have to show for it?"

I tried to stop myself but I busted out laughing. "Taylor you cannot be serious. What do we have to show for it? What 28 year olds do you know that live where we live, drive what we drive, dress the way we dress and can buy what we can buy? We're not out here living paycheck to paycheck. We're good."

"No you're good; I'm not. I wanted more so I took it and I'm not apologizing for it."

"You don't have to apologize for anything. The best apology that you could give me is to grab that pen and sign those papers."
Taylor quickly jumped up from her seat, which caused me to defensively get up out of my seat. She was fuming and I didn't know what she was about to do.
"I'm not signing anything. I leave when I say I'm ready to leave and not a second sooner. You'll just have to kill me first. You got us into this mess and I'm going to see to it that I get US out of it. " Taylor picked up the folder and threw the folder in my direction. If I hadn't ducked out of the way, it would've hit me directly in my face. I watched as the papers flew everywhere around me.
"Are you crazy?" I yelled.
"No I'm not crazy, but you clearly are. You thought you were going to just waltz in here and kick me out of the business that I helped build and I wouldn't leave without a fight? You must not know me as well as I thought."
Before I could respond there was a soft knock on the door behind me. It was Kayla, who stood there with a very worried look on her face.
"Um, is everything okay in here? I could hear you all yelling from the reception area."
Before I could even blink Taylor had walked around the desk and grabbed a decorative paperweight and threw it directly at Kayla.
"Get out of here and mind your business!" Kayla ducked and the paperweight hit the glass door, causing it to shatter into a million pieces. Kayla looked at the glass on the floor and then looked back at us. She looked terrified. She backed out of the office and ran back up to the front.
"Taylor what is wrong with you? You've lost your mind!"
"No you've lost your mind. I can't even stand to look at you right now. I'm out of here. Maybe I'll be back tomorrow, maybe I won't."
Taylor walked back over to the back of the desk and snatched up her purse and cellphone. She stormed out of the office but not before aggressively bumping into me as she walked out. I watched as she stormed down the hallway, flew past Kayla and rushed out of the door. I stood there for a second in a daze. That did not go the way that I planned it in my head at all. I couldn't understand why Taylor was so mad. She wanted out so I spent the rest of our time in Houston with Xavier and his lawyer friend drafting that paperwork to give her what she wanted. I snapped out of my daze and began to

pick up the paperwork off of the floor. As I was putting the paperwork back into the folder, Taylor's computer chimed to notify her that she had a new email. I walked over and jiggled the mouse to log her out and shut the computer down but stopped dead in my tracks once I seen the email address of the most recent email. The email address was desmond.peters@gmail.com. I stood there confused for a moment. What on earth was Desmond doing emailing Taylor? I grabbed the computer chair behind me and sat down. I clicked on the message and opened the email.

Don't worry about it. I'm sure the meeting isn't serious. Just stick to the plan and we'll have Fallon out of our way in no time.

What? What plan? Why would he and Taylor need me out of their way? And what was I in the way of? I was so confused. I scrolled down the email thread as far as I could and began reading. The beginning of the thread was your typical flirting and I quickly learned that they had been sleeping together. Already disgusted, I was about to close her inbox until the word 'kill' caught my eye. I scrolled back a bit and looked at the date of the emails. It was the morning after the Governor's Ball. What I read caused my mouth to drop.

Taylor I think Fallon found out that I'm lying about the Pacers tonight.
What? Why do you think that?
When she pointed out the team owner I didn't know who he was.
I think you're still okay. Just stick to the plan. Hopefully this will all be over soon.
I hope so. I'm ready to get this money and then get out of town ASAP. Do you think she'll put up a fight?
I don't think so. If she does get in the way, we'll just kill her, lol. Call me later. I love you Rocky.

It took everything in me not to grab the computer monitor and throw it against the wall. I was pissed. Had Taylor and Desmond known each other the entire time? In that last message she called him Rocky so she obviously knew more about him than I did. I sat there staring at the screen trying to figure out my next move. I decided that I needed to talk to Desmond face to face. I pressed file and printed off as much of the email thread as I could. I made sure to scroll through the entire the print preview to make sure that I had all of the evidence that I needed just in case he tried to lie when I asked him questions. I got up and grabbed the papers off of the printer and then headed to my office. I grabbed my cellphone and pressed Desmond's name and pressed talk. It rang a couple of times and I was just about to hang up when he finally picked up.

"H-Hello? Fallon?"

"What's up Desmond?"

"Nothing much. I'm surprised to hear from you. You've been ignoring me."

"Yeah, I've just been really busy with work. Would you like to have lunch with me?"

"I'd love to have lunch with you. Where do you want to meet?"

"Hmmm…how about Bakersfield on Mass Ave?"

"Okay. I'll meet you there. How long will it take you to get there?"

"Give me thirty minutes."

"Okay. See you then."

I hung up the phone and then walked up to the reception area to find a still visibly shaken Kayla sitting at her desk.

"Hey Kayla, I wanted to come up here and apologize for Taylor's behavior. We truly value having you here working with us. Taylor and I are having a bit of a personal conflict but we would never drag you into it. How about you take the rest of the day off and we'll start over fresh tomorrow?"

Kayla nodded her head and said, "Okay. Thank you. See you tomorrow."

I turned around to go back to my office and get my purse. I took my time walking through all of the glass on the floor by Taylor's desk. I made a mental note to call the building manager to get that door fixed. I grabbed my purse and made sure that the emails I printed off were neatly folded in there. I walked back up to the front to see Kayla still standing next to her desk fiddling with the pens and pencils she kept in a coffee mug.

"Are you ready to head out Kayla?"

"Yes ma'am. Um, can I ask you something?"

"Of course you can. You don't have to call me ma'am either. I'm not that old."

We both chuckled. "Are you all shutting down the company?"

"No we're not. I promise you, it's just two friends arguing. We began going back and forth and we both got a little emotional. You know how that goes."

"Okay, I was just wondering. It's just that...I really enjoy working here and not to mention the pay is great. I just didn't want to be blindsided if it was closing."

"Trust me, your job is secure."

We got on the elevator and rode down to the lobby in silence. When the doors slid open we both went our separate ways and I headed to my car to make the short drive over to Mass Ave. After circling the block a couple of times to find a parking spot, I finally found one near Bakersfield. I got out of my car and walked into the restaurant. I could see Desmond sitting at one of the wooden lunch tables that they had inside. He had been on his phone but when he glanced up and seen me walking towards him; he quickly put the phone face down and stood up to greet me. *Hmph, he's probably texting Taylor*, I thought to myself. He stood there with a big smile on his face and his arms extended for a hug. I weakly hugged him and I knew he could tell that the happy feeling wasn't mutual. He brushed it off and we both slid into our seats on the wooden benches.

"Well hello beautiful. I'm glad you called me and decided to meet."

"I'm glad you answered. How have you been?"

"I've been okay. I'm better now that you're talking to me again. Is everything okay at work?"

"Yes everything is okay. How are things going at work for you, Daniel?"

"Everything is going okay." At that moment Desmond recognized his mistake and quickly tried to recover. "Wait, what did you call me?"

I smirked at him. "I called you Daniel. That is your real name, isn't it?"

"Look Fallon, let me explain."

"I'm listening."

"It's not what you think. I never meant to hurt you."

"It's not what I think? I think you've been sleeping with my best friend the entire time that you've been with me? Do I have that correct?"

"Fallon...I swear to you that I didn't mean for you to get hurt."

"Trust me; I'm not hurt at all. I knew I should've kept it moving in Miami and never even called you. So what are you and Taylor

—

plotting to do to me? She's already a liar and a thief. What does that make you?"

Daniel cocked his head to the side. "Plotting to do to you? What are you talking about?"

I pulled the emails out of my purse and threw them his way. "You know exactly what I'm talking about. 'If she does put up a fight we'll just kill her'. So both of you were just going to get me out of the picture so you could ride off into the sunset together?"

"Fallon," Daniel placed his head inside of his hands and wiped his face off before resting his chin on his thumbs. "It's not what you think. Give me time to explain."

"You know what? Save it. I don't want to hear anything you have to say. Have a nice life Daniel or Desmond or whatever you're calling yourself today. You two deserve each other." I snatched up my purse and stormed out of the restaurant. As I walked to my car I glanced back inside the restaurant to see Daniel still sitting there with his head cradled inside of his hands. I got even more irritated because he could've at least come running after me. I got into my car and sped away from the restaurant. After I got out of the busy downtown traffic I merged onto the highway and headed towards the fashion mall. I was having such a terrible day; a little retail therapy wouldn't hurt. The highway wasn't too busy so I made it to the mall in record time. I parked in the parking garage and immediately headed to Saks. I spent hours going in and out of all of the stores; trying things on and making impulse purchases just because I could. It got to the point where I had so many bags and boxes that I had to make a trip to my car to put everything away. Once I got to my car I decided not to go back inside the mall but I was a little hungry due to me storming out of Bakersfield before eating earlier. I decided to stop and eat at The Cheesecake Factory. I was seated in a booth near the window and was quickly served my drink and appetizer. What a crazy day it had been. I took a sip of my Georgia peach cocktail and just stared out of the window consumed with my own thoughts. My best friend, someone that I thought loved me and would do anything for me, turned out to be a liar and a thief. My boyfriend, who I had already discovered was a fraud on my own, was sleeping with and working with my so-called best friend to get me out of the way. I couldn't stop thinking about that email. *If she does get in the way, we'll just kill her.* She had said it in a joking manner in the email but there's always truth behind any joke. Would Taylor and Daniel really kill me? After everything they had already done I wouldn't put it past them. The waitress walked over and set my Jamaican black pepper shrimp pasta on the table and told me to be careful because the plate was hot. I thanked her and bent my head down to say grace before I dug in. Before I could really make a dent into the delicious food, my phone rang. It was Xavier requesting to facetime. I accepted the call and as the screen was connecting, I turned on my Bluetooth headset so that nobody sitting around me could hear our conversation.

"Good afternoon Fallon. Are you at your office?"

"Hey Xavier. No, I'm at The Cheesecake Factory right now. My day ended early so I decided to do a little shopping."

"Let me guess, you're eating Jamaican black pepper shrimp with a piece of the salted caramel cheesecake."

"Shows how much you know *Smoke*. I haven't ordered any cheesecake yet."

Xavier laughed at the sound of his nickname from college. "Typical Fallon; you always order the same things."

"I know, I know. It's just that every time I try to try something new I get annoyed by page three of their 200-page menu so I just stick to what I know is good. How's your day going?"

"It's going pretty good so far. How about you? How did the meeting go with Taylor?"

"Man…it went terrible." I grabbed my purse that was hanging from the side of my chair and placed it on the table in front of me. I propped my phone up on the back of my purse so that my hands were free. "It ended with her throwing a paperweight at our receptionist and completely shattering a glass door."

"Wow, really? What went wrong? I thought the final numbers for the buyout worked in her favor?"

"I thought so too. Apparently I was wrong. She kept going on and on about how when she said she wanted out of the business, she meant both of us and not just herself. She said she felt like I was pushing her out of the business."

Xavier shook his head. "Well I seen the numbers from your company evaluation and if that's pushing somebody out then I'd gladly trade her places."

We both laughed. "Yeah well, she has our receptionist completely shook so I just gave her the rest of the day off and took some time to myself as well."

"Well don't worry about it too much. She'll come around eventually."

"Enough about me and my troubles. What's going on with you?"

"Nothing much. I have a big meeting with the chief of police later on but right now I have a little time to myself. You were on my mind so I thought I'd give you a call."

I smiled and flipped my imaginary bang over my eye. "Look at me, getting thought about in the middle of the day and what not."

Xavier rolled his eyes and smiled. "Don't you go getting a big head. I mean, it's already big enough; no need for you to add more weight to it."

"Whatever," I said while laughing. "It was really good seeing you this weekend. I had a lot of fun. It felt like old times."

"Yeah I had a good time too. You know, if you have some free time maybe I could come and visit you up there in Indy soon. I'd love to go back to that donut shop you took me to that one time we were there."

I smiled. "You're talking about Long's. I'd love for you to come up here and visit. I'll give you a real tour of the city this time. We didn't have enough time the first time you came."

"Okay well just let me know your schedule and I'll make time. I'm about to walk into this elevator and it'll probably hang us up so I'll just give you a call later."

"Okay. I'll be waiting." I ended the facetime call and went back to my food. A few seconds later the waitress came back over and asked if I needed anything else. I asked for the check and a slice of salted caramel cheesecake. I couldn't help but smile because Xavier really knew me well. If I weren't in the line of work that I was in we would definitely still be together. Sometimes you have to make sacrifices for the greater good though. I finished my slice of cheesecake, left a tip and then headed out to my car. I slowly drove out of the fashion mall parking lot and then merged onto the highway and headed home. The sun had just begun to set and as I drove I took the time to appreciate all of the beautiful oranges and pinks that the sunset created in the sky. I made it home and pulled into my assigned parking space in the parking lot. I noticed an ambulance and a fire truck and five police cars outside of my building, which was extremely odd. My building was full of young professionals like myself. We were the only ones that would pay as much as we do for one and two bedroom apartments in the middle of the city. There was never any crime or anything like that because for the most part all that we did was go to work and come back home. Someone must have gotten sick or something. When I walked up to the revolving door in the front I was stopped by yellow police tape and a stocky police officer.

"I'm sorry ma'am but we're not letting anybody in this door. This is an active crime scene. Do you live here?"

"Yes I do."

"Do you have an ID or anything that shows your address? We just need to verify that you live here."

I reached into my purse and pulled out my wallet. I pulled out my driver's license and handed it to him. He checked my ID and then handed it back to me.

"Alright ma'am, we're having all current residents enter through the side entrance. We will be out here for a few more hours so please keep that in mind if you order food or need to leave for any reason."

I nodded my head at him in acknowledgment and then began to walk over to the side door. My building was an active crime scene? The most crime that my apartment had ever had was when someone parked in someone else's' assigned parking spot. I made it to the side door and instead of heading to the elevator to go to my apartment. I tried my luck at getting to the front to see if Archie knew anything about what was going on. I made it to the lobby but it was blocked off with police tape too. I ducked under the tape to get a closer look and what I seen stopped me dead in my tracks. There was a policeman taking photos of a body lying in the middle of the floor. A group of police officers were standing next to the body chatting until one of them turned and seen me standing there. He walked over to me and gently grabbed my shoulders.

"Ma'am, I'm sorry but you cannot be down here. You have to go to your apartment until we clean this up and secure the building."

I couldn't move. My entire body was paralyzed and I could barely catch my breath. Archie stared back at me from the floor, lying on his back in a pool of his own blood.

Chapter 8

I stared at the ignition where my push button start was located. My foot was on the brake and my finger was on the button but I couldn't gather up the strength to turn my car on and leave. Archie was gone. I kept seeing his face lying on the ground. His eyes were wide open but the brightness in them that would automatically make me smile was gone. Who on earth would want to hurt Archie? True enough, he looked threatening but he was the sweetest man who would never harm anyone. I could only imagine how his wife and children would take it once they heard the news. After the policeman told me that I couldn't be there, I decided not to go upstairs to my apartment. It just didn't feel right sitting upstairs in luxury while Archie continued to bleed out on the marble floors. I had been sitting in my car for almost an hour. Xavier had called me twice. I sat there and watched the phone ring but I wasn't in the mood to talk right now. Had Archie been fighting someone off? His uniform had still looked starched to perfection like it usually was. Perhaps he had been blindsided and didn't see it coming? No, nothing could get past Archie. He took his job too serious to ever get caught slipping. I wiped the tears from my eyes and finally turned my car on. I pulled out of the parking lot and turned onto the street and headed…where was I headed? I had nowhere to go. I picked up my phone and called Taylor. She was the first person that came to mind and she just so happened to have loved Archie. They always used to joke and flirt with one another. The phone rang once and she sent me to voicemail. I called right back and it went straight to voicemail and didn't even ring. I assumed that she had blocked me. I decided that I was going to pop up on her. She could be mad all she wanted but I really needed a friend right now. I drove over to her apartment and parked my car in the visitor parking area. I quickly scanned the parking lot but I didn't see her car anywhere. I walked into the building anyway and went to the front desk. Her doorman, Henry, was sitting there watching an old episode of Perry Mason on the 13-inch television set that he kept on the counter. I cleared my throat to get his attention and he turned to me and smiled

"Hey Fallon! How's it going?"

"Hey Henry, I'm doing well. How are you? I haven't seen you in a while."

"I know. You've got to come and visit Ms. Smith more often. Speaking of her, you just missed her. She left about five minutes ago with a date."

"Oh did she? This date wouldn't happen to be named Daniel, would it?"

"I'm not really the best at remembering names but I never forget a face. Do you have a picture of him?"

I pulled out my phone and began to scroll through my pictures. "Was this her date?" I handed him my phone so that he could get a closer look at a picture of Daniel.

"Yes ma'am. That's him. He's been hanging around here a lot lately. Do you want me to tell her you stopped by when she gets back?"

"No that's okay. I'm going to give her a call once I get to the car. It was good seeing you again Henry."

"You too Fallon. You be careful getting home."

I started walking back to my car. I wonder how long this thing between Daniel and Taylor had been going on? Obviously long enough for her doorman to know who he was just by looking at a picture. I got in my car and decided to drive past Daniel's house just to see if I could catch them together. It would be pretty hard for them to lie to me or come up with a story with me standing in their face. I tightened my grip on the steering wheel and pressed my foot further down on the gas. The more I thought about the two of them, the angrier I got. I got off on the exit and made my way down Pennsylvania Street to Daniel's apartment. It must have been a Pacers game tonight because the streets were crowded with people and there was traffic everywhere. I turned into the parking garage attached to Daniel's building and found an unreserved spot. I walked to the old rickety elevator and stepped inside and pressed the number four. Before the elevator doors closed all the way I heard a man's voice yelling, "Hold the door!" I placed my forearm in the middle of

---

the elevator doors to stop them from closing and looked out to see a man slowly jogging to the elevator with two overstuffed grocery bags in his arms. He made it into the elevator and immediately sat the bags down and tried to catch his breath.

"Thank you so much. Can you…can you press number four for me?"

"No problem, I'm going to four too."

We made it up to the fourth floor in silence. When we arrived the doors chimed and opened. I stepped into the opening of the doors so they wouldn't close while he got his groceries together. He thanked me again and we both made our way down the hallway. The man continued walking as I stopped in front of Daniel's door but stopped in his tracks when he seen what door I was standing in front of.

"Oh, are you my new neighbor?"

"Um, no. My friend lives here. I was just coming to visit him."

"Are you talking about the tall guy with the long hair?"

"Yes that's him."

"Oh that guy moved out a couple of hours ago. He told us that he was relocating and gave away pretty much everything in his apartment. I told him he was crazy because he gave me a brand new 75 inch TV for free," he said as he laughed. "He didn't tell you he was moving?"

"No he didn't. I guess we're not as good of friends as I thought we were. You have a good night."

I turned around and began walking back to the elevator. What was going on? Daniel really just moved and didn't say a word to me about it. Granted I wasn't speaking to him, but wouldn't you think that that's something you would tell somebody that you claim to care so much about? I felt like I at least deserved a heads up. I pulled out my phone and scrolled to the contact named 'The Man of Your Dreams'. It was so ridiculous to me that I never changed it. I pressed the phone number and the phone rang once.

We're sorry but the number that you have reached is no longer in service. Goodbye.

What? There had to be some kind of mistake. I called the number a few more times but I kept getting the same message. Daniel had cut his phone off. I tried calling Taylor's phone one more time but it was still going straight to voicemail. I was getting more and more frustrated by the minute. As I made my way back to the parking

---

garage to my car, another thought consumed me. That man said Daniel told him he would be relocating. Relocating where? And did Taylor know about him moving? Were they relocating together? I made my way out of the parking garage and back into traffic. I didn't really want to go home but I didn't have anywhere else to go for the night. I thought about getting a room downtown somewhere but decided against it because I didn't feel like spending any unnecessary money. Forget it, I thought to myself. I'll just go home. Before I made my way to the highway I drove over to South Meridian and parked on a metered side street and decided to order a to-go order from Hooter's. I was still kind of full from the Cheesecake Factory that I had earlier but I knew that I probably wasn't going to get any sleep tonight and that I would be hungry later. I sat on a stool at the bar and put in my order of fried pickles, Cajun boneless wings and fries. As I waited, I pulled out my phone and found myself scrolling to Xavier's name. I wanted to call him but I hesitated because what was there to talk about? I had already spoken to him once today and I didn't want to seem worrisome. Swallowing my pride, I pressed talk and listened as the phone rang. Just as I was about to hang up, Xavier finally picked up.

"Well, well, well…today must be my lucky day. I get to talk to you twice in one day."

I laughed. "You're so dramatic. Did I catch you at a bad time?"

"No you're fine. I actually just pulled up at home so you have perfect timing. What's up with you?"

"Nothing…I just…" my voice trailed off.

"What's going on Fallon? You seem stressed out."

"I am stressed out. You know how I told you that the meeting with Taylor didn't go well, right?"

"Yes I remember. Have you talked to her since this morning?"

"No, she's not answering or returning any of my phone calls. But when she left the office I went over to turn her computer off but ended up reading a few of her emails. I found out that she's been doing some other foul stuff too."

"What kind of foul stuff is she doing now?"

"Well," I hesitated. "I haven't been completely honest with you. Before I came down to visit I was seeing somebody before I came. I found out he was lying about who he really was and decided to break it off. I hope you're not mad."

"No I'm not mad. We're not together right now. Do I want that to change in the future? Absolutely. But I can't fault you for something you had going on before we reconnected."

"Wait a minute. Let's go back to the part where you said you're trying to get me back."

Xavier began to laugh. "Let's talk about all of that later. Finish your story. So how did you find out that this guy wasn't who he claimed to be?"

I began telling Xavier the story about the governors' ball and how Daniel ran when the owner of the Pacers came up to speak to me. I told him about everything I found once I googled Daniel's name. I told him how he acted at Bakersfield and how he just moved out of his apartment without a trace.

"Wow, that's insane. He was really living a double life. So what does he have to do with Taylor?"

"Well when I looked on her computer I found emails from him and not only have they been sleeping together this entire time but they've also been plotting to get me out of the way. I don't know exactly what the plan was but Taylor wrote him and told him that if I got in their way they'd just kill me. She said it in a joking way but who would joke about something like that?"

"Oh my God…I don't even know what to say Fallon. Do you want me to put in a call to some people in Indy? If you can get a copy of the email I can make a few calls and get a protection order in place for you so that neither one of them can be in your space."

"No, you don't have to do that. I have protection on me and by me always but thank you though."

"I know this may be too soon for us to be talking about this but have you ever thought about coming back here to Houston? Maybe it's time to get you out of Indianapolis for good."

"I've thought about it but it hasn't gone any further than a thought. Should I be thinking about it?"

"I think you should. I mean I know we just reconnected and we're probably two completely different people than we were before but I never stopped loving you Fallon. I didn't want things to end the first time but maybe they needed to end back then so that we could be having this conversation right now. We had so much fun this past weekend and I haven't been able to stop thinking about you. Would you like to give us another try?"

"I definitely wouldn't be opposed to giving us another try. I didn't want us to end the way we did before either but I felt like my back was against the wall and I had no other choice."

"Yeah I know and let me apologize for that. I should've never given you an ultimatum the way I did. So how about we take things slow and see how they go and lets also work on transitioning you and your business down to Houston? Even if it doesn't work out with us, you'll still always have a friend in me."

"I like that idea. Let's do that."

"Why is it so noisy in your background? Where are you right now?"

"I'm at Hooter's waiting on my to-go order. They're being super slow tonight."

"Let me guess; fried pickles and boneless wings, right?"

I smiled. "I'm sensing some judgment in your voice and I don't appreciate it."

"You're a creature of habit Fallon," he said in between his laughter. "You find something good on the menu and then you never order anything else. I can tell you your order at every food place we've ever been to."

"Whatever. Hold on one second. My food is finally ready." The waitress placed the bag of food on the counter. I thanked her and then headed out of the restaurant and back to my car.

"Okay I'm back. I was thinking about getting a room tonight but I decided to go ahead and go back home."

"What? Get a room? Why would you need to get a room?"

"Oh I forgot to tell you. When I got home from shopping today the police had the lobby of my apartment building blocked off because my doorman got killed."

"Are you serious? Do they know who did it?"

"No and they didn't say anything about catching anyone. I was kind of close to him so seeing him laid out like that has me pretty messed up."

"I'm so sorry to hear that Fallon. I truly am. Man...your life has been like a movie these past few days."

"Tell me about it. I need a vacation."

"Well I'm going to stay on the phone with you until you get home and get settled in, okay?"

"That's cool with me. Thank you Xavier."

Xavier stayed on the phone with me and we joked and laughed my entire ride home. I had indeed given moving back to Houston some thought but I had never made any moves to make it happen. I just always assumed that when all of this was over and I did give this lifestyle up that that was where I was going to end up. With everything going on with Taylor and the future of the company in limbo, it seemed like I would need to make some concrete decisions about relocating. Knowing that Xavier was going to be by my side helping me to get there seemed like an added bonus. I pulled up to my apartment building and all of the police cars, fire trucks and the coroners van were gone. There was still police tape blocking the entrance to the lobby so I walked over to the side door to get in. I peeked around the corner into the lobby and Archie's body was gone but there were a couple of detectives still poking around and taking pictures. I walked over to the elevator and made a mental note to send some flowers to his wife in the morning. When I made it up to my floor I walked down the hall to my apartment. I unlocked the door and made my way inside. The familiar smell of vanilla filled my nostrils and instantly calmed me down. I walked back to my room and sat my purse and keys down and began to get undressed. "Alright Xavier, I made it in safely. I'm about to take a shower and call it a night. I'm worn out."

"Okay. You get you some rest and just give me a call in the morning."

I said goodbye and then tossed my phone on the bed. I finished taking off my clothes and then walked into the bathroom and turned on the shower. I didn't even wait until the water got warm before I jumped in and just stood there for a few seconds. Today had been so stressful. All I wanted to do was get in my bed and go to sleep. I quickly lathered my body with soap and then rinsed off and got out. I put on the terry cloth robe that I kept hanging behind my bathroom door and loosely tied it around my waist. I walked back into the bedroom and the entire room smelled like chicken. I picked up the bag of food that I had sat on the bed and opened up the Styrofoam container. I grabbed a couple of pickles but decided that I was too tired to eat it all and I would save it for lunch tomorrow. I walked to my kitchen and flicked the light on. I opened the right side of my refrigerator and sat the bag in the free space I had on the second shelf. Out of habit, I opened up the left side of the refrigerator, which served as the freezer. I noticed a box of ice cream sandwiches that I had forgotten about and grabbed one to take back to my room with me. I closed the door and there stood a person dressed in all black and a ski mask on staring at me face to face. Before I could scream, the person lunged forward and grabbed me. They covered my face with a damp rag and I was immediately choked up by the smell of it. I kicked and fought as much as I could but I felt my body getting weaker and weaker. All of a sudden, everything went black.

Chapter 9

*A mother and her child are safe and sound after being rescued from
their car during the recent flooding in the third ward. We're live
with the latest update. Also, more rain in the forecast? We'll update
you with more information on more storms heading our way. Good
afternoon everyone, this is KHOU 11 news…*

I slowly opened my eyes and turned to the TV. Why was a Houston
news station on? I groggily began observing the room. I was in a
motel of some sort. I could tell by the tacky yellow tinted lighting
and the outdated patterned on the bedspreads. There were two twin
beds in the room with a nightstand and a lamp in between them. I
was sitting in a chair next to the window but the green paisley print
curtains were drawn. A little sliver of sunlight was peaking in but
not enough to brighten up the room. Once I was fully alert I tried to
move my arms. I tugged and tugged but I couldn't break free from
whatever was holding my wrists. I moved my hands around to see if
it was something that I could fiddle with and untie by myself. It felt
like hard plastic. I assumed it was a zip tie. My entire body was sore
but I continued to try to break free. The afternoon news program on
TV continued on. How did I get to Houston? All I remembered was
being in my kitchen and trying to fight somebody off. I don't
remember anything after that. I looked down at my body. I was still
dressed in my bathrobe and nothing else. My feet were bare and I
desperately needed some lotion. Just then I heard the toilet flush in

the bathroom and I got nervous. I wasn't alone. I heard the bathroom door open and a few seconds later Daniel came around the corner. What was Daniel doing here? He grabbed a bottle of lotion from a black suitcase that was laying on one of the beds and squeezed a little in his hands and began rubbing his hands together. He tossed the bottle back into the suitcase and then casually plopped down on the bed. He picked up the remote and began flipping through the channels. I figured he could sense my eyes burning a hole through him because all of a sudden he turned and stared directly at me. Even in the stale yellow light I could see all of the color drain from his face. He slowly got off of the bed and began walking over to me. I kept my eyes focused on his the entire time. He came and sat directly in front of me and surprisingly, his expression softened.

"Are you okay Fallon? How do you feel?"

I opened my mouth to speak but I sounded extremely hoarse due to not talking for however long I had been knocked out. I tried clearing my throat. Daniel got up and grabbed a paper cup that was sitting on the dresser that held the TV and went to the bathroom. I could hear him turn the faucet on and fill the cup with water. He came back and sat back in front of me.

"Here, drink this Fallon." He put his hand under my chin and then put the cup up to my lips and tilted it towards me so the water could flow into my mouth. The cool water desperately needed to be filtered but it was still refreshing to my dry mouth. Daniel put the cup down and I tried to clear my throat once more. This time when I tried to speak, sound came out.

"Daniel…Daniel, where am I?"

"You're in Houston. Do you remember anything?"

"I remember someone grabbing me in my kitchen. Was that you?"

Daniel nodded his head up and down. "I hadn't planned on hurting you but you didn't make it very easy." He pulled the sleeves of his shirt back and revealed dark bruises and scratches along his forearms.

"You expected me not to put up a fight while you kidnapped me? You're not as bright as I thought. Daniel you…you killed Archie?" Daniel put his head down but nodded yes. "Look, I didn't want to kill him. I asked him to let me upstairs but he gave me a hard time. I wasn't even going to hurt him until he put up a fight and got physical with me."

I felt a tear flow down my face. Archie died trying to do his job and protect me. "You didn't have to do that to him. You could've gotten me another way without hurting him."

"I'm sorry Fallon. It all happened so fast. One minute I was fighting him and the next minute he was on the ground with a gunshot to his head." Daniel reached out to try and wipe the tears off of my face but I quickly snatched away from him. "Don't you dare touch me." Daniel stared at me sadly. "I expected you to be cold towards me. I didn't intend for any of this to happen but you need to listen to me very carefully." He leaned forward and his face became serious. "Fallon I need you to cooperate, okay. I know you're angry and I know how bad you want to put up a fight but I need you to go with the flow until this is all over."

"Daniel what is going on? Why am I here?"

"Listen, I can't tell you everything but I can say that this was not part of the original plan. It wasn't supposed to go down this way."

"Why can't you tell me everything? What plan? Daniel stop playing with me and let me know what's going on."

"Fallon, I want to tell you but I'm trying to keep you safe. The less you know the better. Just do everything that we say and we'll be out of here and back to normal in no time."

"What do you mean we?"

Just then the door opened and a girl with a hood over her head walked in with her hands full of Raising Cane's bags and a drink carrier holding three drinks. She put the food and drinks down and took her jacket off as her long braids swung freely down her back. She turned around and looked at Daniel and me and began to smile. "Well look who finally decided to wake up. Hey Thing 1, are you hungry?"

I stared at Taylor in confusion. My head began to spin. Taylor and Daniel kidnapped me. My best friend and my boyfriend kidnapped me. I could feel the anger building up inside of me but I took heed to Daniel's previous advice and tried to remain calm.

"Taylor, why did you do this to me?"

Taylor walked to the bathroom and washed and dried her hands. She sat down at the table and began to eat her food. She popped a French fry in her mouth and then took a swig of her drink before turning to acknowledge me.

"We haven't done anything to you Fallon. Just do as we say and nobody will get hurt. This time tomorrow we can all go back to Indy worry free."

"What do you mean you haven't done anything to me? You have me tied up in a motel room!"

"Well…you shouldn't have put up such a fight when Rocky tried to take you. I will say that I think we used too much chloroform on her baby. She didn't wake up once the entire drive down here."

Baby. Hearing Taylor call Daniel baby felt like a knife plunged directly into my heart. I turned my head towards Daniel and he wouldn't even look at me. He stared down at his shoes.

"And what is up with you two, Taylor? You've been sleeping with him behind my back this entire time."

"Actually he was mine first," she said as she dipped her chicken strip into the container of dipping sauce. "You were just borrowing him for a little while."

"Borrowing him? How have I been borrowing him?"

"Exactly what I said, borrowing him. Rocky was my boyfriend in high school but we lost touch after I went to TSU and he went to Vanderbilt. We reconnected after he was released from jail and after you began acting so stupid down in Miami, I paid for him to come down and help me out for a little while."

"Help you out with what? Can you speak normally and stop with all of this cryptic mess?'

Taylor took another swig of her drink and then sighed and rolled her eyes. "Okay fine. Look, all of this was not supposed to happen. My original plan was to just get us out of the business. That's all I was trying to do. That's all I've ever been trying to do. Yes, I was taking money on the side. But I was only trying to make sure that I was okay once all of this was over. You were right about me not having any money saved. I had a feeling that Goldie was watching the finances so I decided to give him a show. I assumed that once he seen that the numbers were so low that he would think we couldn't handle the business anymore and take it away from us. We would finally be free! Rocky was only supposed to keep you distracted long enough for you not to notice that the money was coming up missing, not fall head over heels like he did." She cut her eyes at Daniel and he quickly put his head back down.

"So wait a minute…you did all of this to try to get us fired? That was your bright idea? This is the drug game, Taylor. Nobody gets 'fired'."

"Yeah well, my plan would've worked had you been on board from the start. You fought me the entire way and now look at us."

"No it wouldn't. That was a stupid plan that could've gotten both of us killed. The next time you decide to do something like this on your own, do me a favor and don't include me."

Taylor hopped up out of the chair. "Oh like how you included me in your little arrangement with Goldie at the club that night when you got us into this?"

"He was going to kill us! He was going to kill both of us if I hadn't talked him out of it. How many times do I have to explain this? I never wanted to do this either. Who aspires to be a drug dealer, Taylor?"

"Well now the tables have turned in our favor. We're going to kill him."

All of the moisture that was just replenished in my throat disappeared. I squinted in Taylor's direction. "We're going to do what?"

"You heard me. We're going to kill Goldie, after he pays us of course."

Before I could contain it, a small giggle escaped my lips. "You can't possibly believe that you can pull this off. You'll be caught before you get to his front door."

Taylor stared at me blankly. "Don't insult me like that Fallon. Don't make it seem like I'm too stupid to make this happen. Now you're going to cooperate so we can get this done."

"Oh am I? What will happen if I don't?"

Taylor walked over and got directly in my face. "If you don't cooperate then we'll see to it that you'll meet your parents a little sooner than you'd hoped."

I gathered up all of the strength I could muster and charged forward. The chair slid from under me and I went head first into Taylor's chest. She stumbled back a few steps but quickly regained her footing. She rushed towards me and grabbed my shoulders and violently thrust her knee directly into my stomach. All of the wind was immediately knocked out of me. I tried to free my hands one more time so I could get to her like I wanted to but the plastic zip tie would not budge. Daniel leaped off of the bed to separate us. While he pulled Taylor away from me, I used that opportunity to hock up all of the saliva I could and launched it right into Taylor's eye. Taylor stopped in her tracks and wiped the spit from her eye. She looked down at her hand and began to laugh.

"When all of this is said and done, I'm going to kill you myself."

Before I could respond we were interrupted by the sound of a phone ringing. Daniel rushed back over to the bed and fumbled around until he found the small black flip phone.

"Shhhh! You two be quiet now, it's them calling us back. Hello?"

It's who calling them back? I sat there confused and I guess it was written all over my face because Daniel took one look at me and put the phone on speakerphone.

"Good afternoon Rocky. It is Rocky, isn't it? This is Goldie. I got your message. Is Fallon okay?"

"Fallon is fine, Goldie. I'm glad you got the message; do you have my money ready?"

"Before we go any further I want to make sure that Fallon is okay. Can you put her on the phone?"

"My word isn't good enough for you? I said she was okay."

"Actually, it isn't. I don't know anything about you other than the fact that you're demanding ten million dollars from me. Now if you expect to get your money, I need to know that Fallon is okay."

Daniel walked over to me and shoved the phone in my face. "Tell him you're okay. Don't say anything stupid."

I leaned over so that I could speak directly into the phone. "He-hey Goldie. This is Fallon."

"Fallon are you okay? Has he hurt you?"

"I'm okay for now. No, he hasn't hurt me."

"Okay. We're working hard to get you out of there. Before you left did you check your garden?"

Garden? What garden? "I…no I don't think so."

"Remember when you came to visit I gave you the name of that fertilizer for your weeds?"

Just then it clicked. That was Goldie's way of asking about Taylor. I'm assuming he was trying to ask if she was involved. "Yes I do remember. I tried to pull them myself but they ended up taking over the garden anyway."

"That's interesting. Well look, don't worry about it. We'll get your garden taken care of. I'm going to make sure that you make it home safely so that you can do that. Put that guy back on the phone."

Daniel snatched the phone back. "Alright, you see that she's okay. When can I expect my money, Goldie?"

"I want this to be over as quick and as soon as possible. I have your money ready. Where should I meet you, Rocky?"

"I'm going to text you the address. Meet me there in an hour. Look Goldie, no funny business okay? No police, no extra people. Make the drop alone."

"Rocky, I know you don't know me very well but don't insult me by assuming that I would involve the police. I have been extremely cooperative up to this point but don't piss me off by trying to be tough."

Daniel laughed. "I'm not about to go back and forth with you, old man. Just have my money ready when I see you." He flipped the top of the phone down and hung up. He then opened the phone back up and text the address to Goldie.

"Alright ya'll, it goes down in an hour. Let's get this money!" Taylor hopped up and walked over to the suitcase. She dug around for a while and then pulled out a black long sleeved shirt and a pair of black leggings. She walked to the bathroom to change clothes. Daniel already had on black pants but he walked over to the suitcase shortly after Taylor and pulled out a black shirt for himself. He slipped on some black Timberland boots and I noticed another smaller pair sitting on the floor next to the bed. I knew that I should be scared but surprisingly, I wasn't. Taylor and Daniel were trying to pull off their little Bonnie and Clyde act but judging by how frantic and hurried their movements were around this room, I could tell that they were terrified. I also wasn't too worried because I knew Goldie; there was no way he was going to come by himself and drop off that much money. He may have been small in stature but he was very crafty and wasn't to be underestimated. Deep down inside I knew I was going to be okay. Just then, my stomach began to growl. I couldn't even remember the last time that I had eaten anything.

"Daniel, can I please have something to eat?"

Daniel looked at me with an uneasy stare. "Can't you just wait until all of this is over?"

"Please Daniel. I haven't had anything since before you took me. Please, I'm starting to feel sick."

Daniel let out a groan and then walked over to the table. He picked up one of the Raising Canes containers and a drink and brought it over to me.

"Are you planning to sit here and feed me like a child? You have to release my hands," I said and wiggled my arms back and forth.
"No, you're going to have to figure it out. I can't let you free."
"Look Daniel, you said it's almost over. I'm not going to try anything crazy. I just want to eat."
Daniel stared at me for a few seconds and then walked over and picked up his keys. There was a small utility knife on his key ring and he walked behind me and used that to cut through the zip tie. I stretched my arms and began to massage my wrists. The little tousling match with Taylor made the zip tie cut through my skin so there was a little pain and discomfort but luckily it didn't go deep enough to draw blood. I focused my attention on the food. It had gotten cold but you would think that it was a gourmet meal. I hadn't eaten in so long. I scarfed down the chicken and fries like a savage. Taylor walked out of the bathroom and seen me eating and froze.
"You freed her hands?"
"Calm down Taylor. She's not going to do anything. Let her eat. She hasn't eaten anything in two days."
I had been knocked out for two days? How much chloroform had they used? I kept my thoughts to myself and kept eating. I figured it was best that I kept quiet and just went along with the program. As I ate, I sat and watched Taylor load the clip into a black 9 mm handgun and place it in the small of her back. Daniel was sitting on the bed loading two silver .45 caliber handguns. It wasn't until I seen the guns that I got nervous. Taylor put on a leather jacket and picked up a small black duffel bag. She tossed it over to me.
"Here's your stuff. Get dressed. When we make the drop, keep the bag in the car. As soon as we get finished with Goldie we're getting on the road."
I unzipped the bag. Inside were my phone, my purse and a change of clothes. I checked my purse and everything was still intact; nothing was missing from my wallet and all of my cards and IDs were there. Daniel and Taylor quickly stuffed all of their clothes and other belongings into the black suitcase on the bed. Daniel zipped the suitcase and carried it to the door. Taylor grabbed all of the trash from the food and then came and grabbed my trash. She picked up the drink and noticed that it was full and then handed it back to me.
"Here, bring this with you."
I obliged and stood up. I immediately sat back down. My legs felt like cement blocks and wouldn't budge. I don't know how long I had

been sitting in the chair but my legs were clearly out of practice and me lunging towards Taylor so abruptly didn't help at all. Taylor rolled her eyes and sucked her teeth as she grabbed my arm and helped me up. I slowly began to take steps to the bathroom. "Fallon you're going to have to walk by yourself when we get outside. I don't want anyone around here getting suspicious." I nodded my head at her in acknowledgement. I slowly walked into the bathroom and closed the door behind me. I took a look at myself in the dirty bathroom mirror. I looked a mess. My hair was all over the place. My face was ashy and my eyes were bloodshot red. I turned on the faucet and quickly splashed my face with water. I grabbed a washcloth from the stack on the back of the toilet and dried off. I looked in my purse and found a small comb. I used that and a little bit of water to comb my hair down into a quick style. Thank God for this pixie cut, I thought to myself. I dug around in my purse a little more and found a tube of lip-gloss. I quickly put it on and smiled. I still looked bad according to my own standards but it would have to do for now. I pulled out the clothes Taylor had obviously taken from my house. There was a long sleeve black shirt and a pair of black leggings like her. Taylor and Daniel were doing a terrible job at being inconspicuous because we all had on black. If I were just a stranger on the street and I seen us coming, I would automatically be tipped off that something was up. Taylor began banging on the door yelling for me to hurry up. I got dressed as fast as I could and slipped on the boots that were in the bag. After taking one more look in the mirror, I walked back and joined Taylor and Daniel. Daniel turned off the light in the room and Taylor opened the door. The sunlight immediately blinded me and I took a moment to breathe in the fresh air. I looked around observing my surroundings. We were at a rest stop of some sort; there was a BP and a Sunoco across the street, a McDonald's on the left side of the motel and a KFC on the right. Taylor walked over to the dumpster in the corner of the parking lot and threw away all of the trash that we had in the room. As she walked back Daniel led me to a rented silver Chrysler 300 and opened the back door for me. I slid into the backseat as he and Taylor got in the front. We pulled out of the parking lot and immediately got on the interstate. I paid attention to the signs on the side of the road and it looked like we were on the outskirts of the city. Daniel had his phone propped on the dashboard. I tried to pay attention to the GPS but it was hard to see from the backseat. We drove for another ten minutes before we got to the Baytown area of the city. This particular area housed a lot of industrial and office buildings. There were also a number of development properties that were in the process of being built but weren't completed. We pulled up to one of the incomplete properties and parked. I looked around and didn't see any other cars around. There was construction equipment all around the place. It looked like the only thing that had been built so far was the foundation and very little else.

"Do you think he's already here?"

Daniel looked at his phone. "He should be. I told him an hour."

Like clockwork, the black flip phone began to ring.

"Hello?"

"Mr. Rocky, is this you in the silver Chrysler?"

"Yeah that's me. Where are you?"

"I'm already inside. I'm a stickler for being on time."

"Okay. Here we come."

Daniel hung up the phone and looked over at Taylor. She grabbed his hand.

"This is it baby. It's finally over." She squeezed his hand and then leaned in for a kiss. Daniel leaned over and met her halfway. They kissed each other passionately and completely forgot that I was in the backseat. The only thing that stopped me from punching both of them in the head was the fact that they had guns. After they came up for air, they both hopped out of the car and Daniel opened the door for me and let me out. We walked into the building. The floor was concrete so we kicked up dust as we walked. The building was still in the beginning stages; there were areas marked off showing where different offices were going to be and there were construction lifts in every corner of the room because they had begun building the second floor. Goldie was standing in the middle of the building with two big black duffle bags on either side of his body. He stood there expressionless and with his hands clasped in front of his body. We stopped walking about twenty feet in front of where Goldie was standing.

"Well if it isn't the infamous Goldie. It's so nice to finally meet you."

"It's nice to meet you too Rocky. It's too bad that it has to be under these circumstances. Taylor you're just going to stand there and not speak? I thought we were better than that."

Taylor looked down at her shoes and mumbled softly, "How you doing Goldie?" For this to be her master plan, she sure wasn't confident at this very moment.

"I wont lie to you; I've been better. Fallon are you okay?"

I nodded my head. "Yes I'm fine Goldie."

"See? I told you I wouldn't hurt her. I keep my promises. Now let's see if you keep yours. Is all of the money there?"

"It's all there; all ten million American dollars. So how are we going to do this?"

"Taylor is going to come and get the bags from you and we're going to check and make sure that the money is there and that it's real. After we check it, Fallon can walk over and we can go our separate ways."

"That seems fair. Come on Taylor," Goldie said and motioned for her to walk over.

Taylor slowly began to walk over to Goldie. Something in the corner of the room caught my eye. On one of the construction lifts I noticed what looked like a crumpled up pile of tarp on top of it. I stared at the tarp as Taylor walked over. It seemed so out of place. Taylor made it over to Goldie and picked up the bags off of the ground. She didn't look at Goldie once. The bags were heavy so she struggled to walk on the way back. When she finally made it back over, Daniel pulled out his gun and pointed it in Goldie's direction. Taylor bent down and checked the bags of money. Daniel kept the gun pointed at Goldie while also trying to focus on Taylor and the money. While Daniel had his head down looking into the bags, Goldie got my attention and tilted his head in the direction of the construction lift that I was looking at previously. I focused back on the tarp. What was that up there? It wasn't flat on the ground; it was bunched up into a pile. It's not out of the ordinary for there to be tarp on a construction site. It just didn't make sense for it to be up there on that lift. Both Taylor and Daniel quickly stood upright after zipping up the bags.

"It's real. I'm going to assume that it's all there. You'd be a fool to try any funny business right now. It's been a pleasure doing business with you, boss." Daniel grabbed my arm and pushed me forward. I stumbled to the front and began walking towards Goldie. Goldie stared at me blankly as I made my way to him. When I got halfway there I heard Taylor calling my name.

"Hey Fallon!"

I turned around halfway. "Yes?"

"You should really think the next time you spit in somebody's face," she said and then quickly pulled her gun from her back and pulled the trigger.

The bullet slammed into my chest and I fell to the ground. Everything began to move in slow motion. As I fell I seen the tarp on top of the construction lift fly back and Bentley hopped up and began firing an assault rifle. Tone came from behind one of the concrete doorways that had been blocked off for an office and began shooting his pistol as well. I tried to forget the pain that was coming from my chest and gathered myself in the fetal position to take cover. I felt someone grab my arm and Goldie yelled, "Come on Fallon! Get up! Get up!" I looked up and it was Tone grabbing me and dragging me to my feet. Bentley was still firing shots and I turned to see Taylor's body shaking from the multiple bullets piercing through her body. Daniel was hit in his leg and in his shoulder but he still grabbed the bags of money and struggled to run out of the building and return shots in Bentley's direction. He ran out of the door and Taylor's body finally collapsed onto the ground. Bentley stopped shooting. I don't know what came over me but I struggled to run over to her. I dropped down to the ground and put her head in my lap. Her lifeless eyes stared back at me. I sobbed loudly and began to scream. My best friend was gone.

Chapter 10

"Fallon baby, come on. We have to go. I know you're hurting but we have to get out of here."

I was still on the ground holding Taylor. I held her head in my lap and rocked back and forth as tears continued to flow from my eyes. She was really gone. Goldie walked over and gently put his hand on my shoulder. I looked up at him through the tears.

"Fallon, she's gone. Let her go. Come on."

I placed my hand over her face and closed her eyes. I gently laid her head down on the ground and kissed her on her forehead. Tone grabbed me by my arm and helped me up off of the ground. The adrenaline was wearing off in my body and I began to feel all of the pain from the gunshot. Luckily for me Taylor had bad aim. She shot me on the right side of my chest, almost high enough for it to have hit my shoulder. Tone could see that I was struggling to walk by myself so he picked me up and carried me to the truck. They had parked behind the building next to where we had met up. Bentley ran to get the truck while Tone and Goldie stayed with me. Tone took off his shirt and tied it around my collarbone to try and stop the bleeding. Bentley pulled up to us and Goldie opened the back door of the truck as Tone gently laid me down on the seat. Goldie hopped in the front seat and Tone slid in the back with me.

"Fallon I know you're in pain but hold on a little longer until we get to the house, okay?"

I weakly nodded my head at Goldie. I was so tired. I just wanted to close my eyes and go to sleep. I was in so much pain that I couldn't even muster up any tears. I kept my eyes open as long as I could so I wouldn't alarm them.

"I knew I should've shot both of them as soon as they walked in there. I could've gotten them both if I was able to use my scope. I'm sorry boss." Bentley slammed his hands against the steering wheel over and over again until Goldie grabbed his right arm to calm him down. Bentley took a few deep breaths and calmed himself enough to be able to start driving again.

"Don't beat yourself up about it Bentley. We just wanted to get Fallon out of there safely and we did that as best as we could. You didn't know that Taylor was going to start shooting. After we get Fallon cleaned up and taken care of, we're getting Rocky and we're getting my money back. If I have anything to do with it, he won't be leaving the state of Texas breathing."

"Don't you worry about him, boss. I put trackers in both of the bags back at the house. He may think he's gotten away but I've got my eye on him," Bentley said as he handed Goldie his phone. From where I was laying I could see a little bit of the screen and it looked like Goldie was looking at a regular GPS but it showed a car going in the opposite direction of us. Goldie handed the phone back to Bentley and smiled. He then picked up his own phone and began to make a call.

"Dr. Wallace? Hello there, this is Goldie. I'm doing well, how are you? How are the kids? Draya is great, just as beautiful as always. Listen, I need a big favor from you and it's an emergency. I have someone that requires medical attention but we can't take her to the hospital. Can you meet me at my house? Yes, it's a gunshot wound. Thank you so much. Fifteen minutes? Fifteen minutes is great. See you then."

Goldie hung up the phone and turned back to face me. "Fallon I need you to hold on for fifteen more minutes. Can you do that for me?" I slowly nodded my head yes and fought to keep my eyes open. I was so tired. Bentley continued to drive down the highway. I turned my head and looked at Tone. He was silently staring out of the window but he turned and looked at me. He curled his lips into a slight smile and then grabbed my hand and squeezed it. He held my hand for the rest of the ride. A few minutes later we pulled up to Goldie's estate. Tone hopped out of the truck and then slowly slid me out of the backseat and carried me like he would carry his bride over the threshold. Before we could make it to the door, Draya swung the side door open and ran over to me.

"Oh my God, what happened to her? Fallon are you okay? Baby is she going to be okay?"

Goldie calmly walked over to her. He wrapped his arms around her waist and ran his fingers through her hair to calm her down. "She's fine Draya. Dr. Wallace is on his way over here and he's going to get her together. She'll be back to normal in no time."

Tone carried me through the door and led me to Goldie's office. He laid me down on the leather couch and then sat down in one of the chairs in front of the desk and put his head in his hands. Bentley grabbed the other chair next to him and walked it over to the door and posted up there. He continued to look at his phone screen tracking Daniel. Bentley didn't really know me that well but Tone had known me since I was 18 so he was taking this extremely hard. Just then Goldie walked in with a tall white man with neatly groomed red hair and a matching red beard. He wasn't dressed like a normal doctor; he had on a dress shirt, skinny ankle length slacks, suspenders and Brook's Brothers slip on velvet loafers. He was carrying a large black bag. He walked over to me and smiled.

"Hello there beautiful. My name is Dr. Wallace. It looks like you've gotten into a little accident, huh?"

I weakly nodded my head yes.

"Well I'm going to examine you a little and then we're going to get you stitched up and back to 100%, okay? Can one of you all do me a favor and help me lift her up?"

Tone walked over and gently propped me up on the couch so that I was sitting upright. Dr. Wallace began to examine the wound. He opened the black bag and pulled out something that looked like a large price scanner and gently placed it against the wound. I winced and cried out in pain. Tone looked at me and shook his head and then quietly walked out of the room.

"Well you're one lucky lady; the bullet went straight through. I'm going to stitch this up and give you something that will help the pain and you'll be back to new in no time."

I cleared my throat and asked him, "Is it okay for me to go to sleep now?"

Dr. Wallace chuckled and nodded his head yes. "Let me give you something that will make you more comfortable." He reached into the bag and pulled out a small container filled with bottles of medicine. He picked out one of the bottles and then grabbed a small plastic packet that held a syringe inside. He pulled out a pair of gloves and an alcohol swab. He rolled up my sleeve on my right arm and wiped the inside of my arm with the alcohol swab. "You're going to feel a little pinch, okay?" I nodded and Dr. Wallace stuck the syringe into my arm. He cut the rest of my blood soaked shirt off and began working on my wound. I tried to stay up and watch him work but my eyes began to get heavy and within two minutes, I was out like a light.

I woke up the next morning in a daze. It took me a few minutes to realize where I was. Once I looked over and seen the wall of books in Goldie's office, the memory of what happened rushed to my head and I began to panic. I called out for Goldie. Tone rushed into the room and tried to calm me down. I stopped yelling for Goldie but I was still visibly shaken. Whatever Dr. Wallace had put on my wound was still working because I wasn't in too much pain but I still wasn't able to move my right arm without being uncomfortable. Goldie walked in and smiled at me.
"How are you feeling, Fallon?"
"I'm okay. I'm still a little groggy though. I'm not in too much pain. I'm starving."
"Okay. Chef Warren has already made breakfast. Do you think you can walk? If not I'll bring your plate in here."
"I think I can make it to the kitchen."
Tone grabbed my elbow and slowly guided me up off of the couch. I took short, stuttered steps but somehow I made it from Goldie's office all the way down the hallway to the kitchen. Chef Warren was up fixing a plate of waffles with fruit and fried potatoes. When he noticed me walking in he smiled and said, "There she is. You made it just in the nick of time." As Tone helped me into my seat, Chef Warren walked over and placed the plate of food in front of me. He walked back to the refrigerator and pulled out a bottle of orange juice. He poured me a glass and came back over and sat it in front of me. I thanked him and began to dig in. Goldie, Bentley and Tone came and joined me at the table. They were quiet at first but Goldie broke the silence.
"Fallon, I know you're in a lot of pain but we can't let that Rocky character get away with this. I'm not worried about the money but I'll be damned if he doesn't feel some type of pain for what he and Taylor did to you. Now we've been tracking him all night and he's

stopped at a little motel right outside of Pasadena. We need your help in getting him. Will you help us out?"

I finished chewing my food before answering. "Can I pull the trigger?"

Tone shook his head no. "I don't think that's a good idea. You may not remember because you were sedated but you had nightmares off and on last night about Taylor and were talking and crying in your sleep. I don't think you're built for that."

"We are not planning on killing him. But we have to be cautious in our approach. Now if he's a smart man then he is going to be on the lookout for these two and me. He's not going to expect to see you. If anything he thinks you're dead. We already have a plan for what we want to do but we need you to approach him in order for our plan to work. You'll be able to distract him long enough for us to get it done. Now all we need right now is a reason for you to meet with him."

I picked up another piece of waffle and began to chew as I thought about what I could do to get close to Daniel again. I wanted to call him and curse him out one last time but I didn't have my phone. Just then, a light bulb went off in my head.

"My bag!"

All three men stared at me, puzzled because of my random outburst. "What about your bag?"

"I left my bag in the car before we walked in to meet Goldie. It has my phone, my purse, ID's, credit cards and everything else in there. Taylor told me to leave it in the car because…" I stopped myself once I remembered their original plan.

"Because what?"

"Because…they were going to take the money and kill you. She told me to keep my bag in the car because after we left we were getting straight on the road back to Indiana."

"Well," Goldie said as he twirled his goatee. "We see how that plan turned out." All three men began to laugh. I sat there emotionless. I still couldn't believe Taylor was actually gone. "Okay so now that we have a reason for you to contact him, I need you to call him. Can you do that for me?"

"Yes, I can. Whose phone am I going to use?"

Bentley pulled a Wal-Mart bag from under the table. He handed it over to me and I looked inside. There was a Straight Talk Wireless flip phone with a 45-minute calling card inside. "I went and got this last night. You'll use this to communicate with him until our plan is in place. I've already programmed his number in there for you."

I took the phone out of the bag and went to the contacts. It had been a long time since I'd had a flip phone so it took me some time to figure out how to use it again. I pressed talk and then put the phone on speaker and set it on the table. The phone rang twice before Daniel picked up.

"Hello?"

"Daniel, this is Fallon. Don't hang up."

I was met with complete silence. The only way I knew that he was still there was the sound of the television he had blaring in the background.

"F-Fallon listen me, I'm so sorry. I didn't know that she was going to do that. You have to believe me."

"I don't know what or who to believe anymore. I'm calling you because I need to get that duffle bag with my things in it from you. I left it in the backseat."

Daniel was quiet for a second then began to laugh. "You must think I'm stupid. Goldie! Where's Goldie?" He began yelling into the phone. "Goldie if you want it with me then you come and get me yourself. Don't have your little minions calling me to try and set me up." Goldie sat up in his chair and opened his mouth to respond but I quickly shook my head no and put my hand up to stop him.

"Daniel, what are you talking about? Goldie is nowhere around me. They dropped me off at the hospital and basically left me for dead. I'm out here with no phone, no wallet, no ID and no money. All I want is to get my things from you so that I can get home and get away from all of this mess." I raised my voice and had begun crying. "Can I please meet you somewhere or you can just drop it off and leave it somewhere and I'll come and get it. Don't leave me out here with nothing like this, please." I sobbed even harder into the phone.

"Fallon, baby, please stop crying. I didn't mean for any of this to happen. You know I love you. I have always loved you. This whole thing, it just…it just spiraled out of control. I'll bring you your things. Where do you want to meet?"

"I'm staying with my friend in the fourth ward. You can meet me at Sam Houston Park. I'll be standing at the red and white gazebo. It's right in the middle of the park. You can't miss it. Is 4 o'clock okay?"

"4 o'clock is fine."

123

"Oh my God, thank you Daniel." I began crying again. "You're a lifesaver."

"Fallon please stop crying. I hate to hear you like this. Look everything is going to be okay. I'll see you in a few."

I hung the phone up and wiped the tears from my eyes. I looked up at Goldie, Tone and Bentley and smiled before taking another sip of my juice and rolling my eyes. "Ugh, are you sure we can't just kill him?"

Chapter 11

I stood at the gazebo and looked out at the small manmade lake running through Sam Houston Park. I took a look up and gazed at the skyscrapers that surrounded the park. It always made me laugh how this quaint and quiet little park was right in the middle of all of the hustle and bustle of the city. I turned around and looked out at the parking lot that led to where I was standing and could see Draya sitting in the car keeping watch and waiting for Daniel to pull up. We decided to have Draya drive me to the park. Daniel knew what all of the men looked like and we needed this plan to work. He had never seen Draya before and I had said over the phone that I was staying with a friend. I turned back around and focused my attention on a gaggle of geese waddling around near the water. I must have been staring at them for longer than I thought because I didn't even notice when Daniel walked up behind me.

"Hey Fallon."

I spun around a little too fast and instantly regretted it as I winced in pain. Daniel looked exhausted; his eyes were sunken in and his hair was all over the place. He had on jeans, but the left pant leg was bulging because of whatever he had wrapped his gunshot wound with. He had wrapped the gunshot wound on his shoulder with a black t-shirt. I assumed that as a precaution he had taken his medical care into his own hands because a hospital would've alerted the police. He held the small black duffle bag in his left hand and a silver pistol in his right.

"Hey. What do you need that for?" I asked and pointed at the gun.

"Protection. I didn't know what to expect. You have every right to do something crazy to me."

I shook my head. "I already told you, I am just here to get my bag so that I can go home."

Daniel walked closer to me. "Can we sit somewhere and talk?"
I took a look around the park and noticed a bench not too far from
the gazebo. "Sure. Let's go over there."
I made sure to walk in front of Daniel so that I could sit at the far
edge of the bench. At that angle I could still see the parking lot.
Daniel took a little longer to get to the bench because he was
walking with a limp. When he finally arrived he slowly sat down and
for a few moments, we sat in silence. Once he had sat down Draya
waited a few seconds to make sure I had his undivided attention. She
slowly got out of the car and began trying to get his trunk open.
"Fallon, I just want you to know that I never meant to hurt you. I
never should've agreed to do anything with Taylor in the first place
but I just got in too deep too fast and before I knew it, it was too
late."
"Can I ask you something?"
"You can ask me anything."
"Let's say I did eventually come around and go with the program.
You were dealing with both me and Taylor; how were you going to
choose who you wanted to be with in the end?"
Daniel took a deep breath and leaned forward with his hands clasped
in front of him. He was careful to put all of his weight on his
uninjured leg. I took that opportunity to look out at the parking lot. I
could see Draya had finally got the trunk of Daniel's car opened and
began going to work.
"To be honest with you Fallon, I don't know. I thought about that
often. I just assumed I would deal with that when the time came."
I sucked in my teeth and shook my head. "Was anything about you
and me real?"
Daniel looked at me with a hurt expression on his face. "Yes it was
real, Fallon. I may have lied to you about who I was and what I did
for a living but my feelings for you were real." He grabbed my right
hand gently so he wouldn't pull my arm and bring me any pain. "I
love you Fallon. I always will."
I looked him in the eye and he seemed genuine. I slowly snatched
my hand away. "Well it's too bad that I can't say the same."
Daniel bit his bottom lip and put his head back down. I looked out at
the parking lot and Draya was closing Daniel's trunk and putting the
big bags of Goldie's money into the trunk of our car. I waited until
she was safely back in the car before I spoke again.

"Well Daniel, this little meet up has been fun but my pain medicine is starting to wear off and I need to lie down."

"Okay well let me at least walk you to the car."

I panicked a little bit but went ahead and let him walk me to the car. Draya had already put the moneybags in the trunk so nothing about our car looked suspicious. When we got to the car he opened the door for me and I slid inside. He leaned down on the passenger door so that he could speak to Draya.

"Hello, how are you doing? My name is Daniel." He reached inside the car and extended his hand to her.

Draya put on a smile and shook his hand. "Hey Daniel, my name is Ashley. Fallon, girl he is gorgeous. Where have you been hiding him?"

I laughed it off and turned to Daniel. "Well…it was nice knowing you."

Daniel placed his hand over his heart and tugged at his chest while laughing. "Man, you've always been so cold. But I understand. I'll see you around Fallon."

You won't, I thought to myself but I smiled and waved at him as he got into his car. He quickly put the car in reverse and sped off. As he drove off I noticed his back taillight was broken, just as we planned. I turned to Draya.

"Did you get everything done?"

Draya nodded her head yes. "I got it done. I should've shot him in the face when I had the chance for trying to kill my husband but I stuck to the plan."

I smiled and reached into the duffle bag and pulled out my phone. It was dead. I plugged it into the car charger and waited for it to power up. "Good. Let's get out of here." Draya made her way out of the parking lot and we headed back to the estate.

I must have gotten back to the house and went straight to sleep because the next morning Goldie gently shook me awake in the guest bedroom.

"Fallon…Fallon baby, wake up. I've got a surprise for you."

I opened my eyes and slowly propped myself up against the headboard. The pain meds Dr. Wallace had given me were wearing me out. I was still a little groggy but I perked up because usually when Goldie has a surprise, it's a good one.

"What's the surprise Goldie?"

Goldie clicked on the TV in the room and turned the channel. One of the local news stations was on. "You'll see in a minute."
The news was reporting the 7-day forecast. After the meteorologist finished up her report the camera cut back to the two news anchors at the desk.

...And now for an ABC 13 breaking news exclusive. What started off as just a routine traffic stop for a broken taillight ended in police making an arrest for drug trafficking. Police arrested 29-year-old Daniel Peters after a routine traffic stop led to them finding five kilos of cocaine and two unregistered firearms in the trunk of a rental car. Police were alerted to check the vehicle after the first officer on the scene noticed the smell of marijuana coming from inside once the suspect rolled the window down. The suspect has not been formally charged but he is facing five counts of possession with the intent to distribute a controlled substance, two counts of possession of a fire arm without a license, driving with a suspended license and resisting arrest. He is being held with no bond...

I turned to face Goldie. He was still staring at the TV with a look of satisfaction on his face.
"Wow. I thought you all were going to kill him."
"I thought so too. At first I wanted nothing more than to see him lying on the ground pleading for his last breath but then I had a change of heart. I figured it would give me much more satisfaction to know that he was somewhere rotting in a cage so I filled the car up with enough drugs and guns to make sure he was put away forever. Not to mention I have enough friends on the inside from guards to inmates that will make sure that anywhere that he ends up won't be a pleasant stay." We both laughed. We continued watching the news in silence before Goldie spoke up again.
"You know Fallon, I'm tired."
"I'm tired too. Those painkillers Dr. Wallace gave me are no joke."
"No I don't mean physically tired, I mean mentally. I've been doing this a long time."
"I know you have. Look at those wrinkles," I said as I playfully pointed at Goldie's face. He swatted my hand away. "Whatever. You know I still look good." He ran his hands through his curls and I responded by rolling my eyes.

"No but seriously, for me to be around for this long and to have all of this is truly a blessing. I mean. I started off in middle school on the corner selling joints of sherm. There were many others that started out with me that are locked up or dead. I'm thankful to be here but I am tired."

The look on Goldie's face made me sit up straighter. "Goldie what's going on?"

Goldie looked over at me and smiled. He got up off of the bed and began fiddling with the small figurines that they had as decoration on top of one of the dressers.

"You know that I've never had children? I've never really had the desire to and we all know that Draya isn't messing up her body to have any. But lately I've begun thinking about who would all of this go to whenever I decided to throw in the towel." He walked over to the window and began looking out. "This probably isn't the best time to ask you this but…Fallon, how much do you like running your business?"

"You're right Goldie. This is horrible timing." We both laughed. "I mean…I guess I could say that I like it. It is nerve-racking at times whenever we get extremely high profile clients like the governor but that just comes with the nature of the business. I love all of the perks the job gives me. I'm always being sent free tickets to events and flowers and things like that."

Goldie slid back on the dresser and had a seat. "I know Taylor's excuse for causing all of this turmoil was because she wanted out. Do you want out?"

"Honestly Goldie, I never thought about it until she kept bringing it up. I was fine with my life and the lifestyle that I was living. And you made it very easy for us. We never had to stand on the corner. I've never had to sit and measure anything out on a scale. And even if we were put in a situation where we had to go to the hood to make drop offs or anything like that, we always had Tone with us. I always said that once I got married and started a family I was going to stop doing it. After that whole ordeal with Daniel, I think I'm good on relationships for a while now though." Goldie and I both shared a laugh.

"Look Fallon, I'm not going to beat around the bush any longer. I can't do this forever. I have thought long and hard about this and I've made a decision. I want you, only if you're willing of course, to succeed me. Since day one you've proven to be loyal to me and you're the closest thing I have to a daughter."

"Goldie...I..."

Goldie held his hand up in protest. "Now you don't have to give me an answer right now. I expect you to take some time to think about it. I just wanted to bring what I've been thinking about to your attention."

"Goldie are you sure? I mean, what do you plan on doing...just walking away from all of this completely?"

"Not at first. Of course I'll be one call away to guide you and teach you everything there is to know but eventually, yes. I want a clean slate."

"What about Draya?"

"Draya is on board. So are Tone and Bentley. I've talked to all of my people and they're big fans of you. A lot of people out here respect you and the way you move and do business. Pretty much everyone that I've discussed this with agree that the only person that can handle this job is you."

"Goldie I just...I don't know what to say. What are you going to do now?"

Goldie fiddled around with his ever-present gold watch on his wrist. "I don't know yet. Travel the world. Move to another state and completely start over. You know what they say; sometimes you've got to go where nobody knows your name."

"This is how I know you're getting old. That is not how the song goes." We both erupted into laughter.

"Listen...I don't expect for you to give me an answer right this second but I will need one pretty soon. I'll leave you alone and give you some time to think."

Goldie walked out of the room. I sat there for what seemed like forever thinking about what he just said. Goldie was really considering giving this entire business to me. This wasn't like before when Taylor and I started our little company. I was about to be in charge of pretty much the entire state of Texas, some of Louisiana and a good portion of the Midwest too. Just the thought of all of the people that would have to answer to me caused me to break out into a sweat. I carefully got out of bed and walked to the bathroom to prepare for a shower. Dr. Wallace had told me to steer clear of showers and just sponge off until I got my stitches removed but a shower always makes me feel better. I would just have to be careful not to get the gauze covering my stitches wet. As I stood there, awkwardly with one arm in the shower and one arm out, the water beating against my body instantly relaxed me. I tried to cool down and let the stress of the past couple of days get washed down the drain. I started out selling drugs when I was 18. Sure in the beginning it was all about survival and making sure that I could support myself but as more money began to flow, the more comfortable I became. I have never been the type of person that was easily trusting of people but if you would've told me that Taylor would've went through all of the lengths that she did to bring the business, and eventually us down, I would've ignored her in the food court that day. If you would've told me that my best friend would've been the one to pull the trigger and try to kill me, I would've struck a deal with Goldie in the club that night to only save myself and not the both of us. After all that I've been through, for me to be still standing was remarkable. A weird feeling came over me when I thought about my last meeting with Daniel. The thought that I had the upper hand in that situation without him having any clue made me feel...powerful. The feeling was unlike anything I had ever felt before. I knew what it was like to have money. I had been in a position to buy whatever I wanted whenever I wanted for a long time but this feeling of power was new to me. I'm ashamed to admit how much I liked it. I was never one to follow; I've always been a natural born leader. I marched to the beat of my own drum. Knowing all of the people that would have to answer to me excited me but it also made me nervous. How would they feel about me running things? I already knew that having to answer to a woman might be an issue to some but would everybody feel that way? All of this thinking and worrying had not only given me a headache, but the awkward way that I had to stand in the shower had caused my wound to begin to hurt again. I turned the water off and got out of the shower. I applied body butter to my body and carefully put on the clothes that Draya had went out and gotten me the day before. I walked over to the side of the bed and grabbed the medicine bottle that was on the nightstand. I popped two of the painkillers into my mouth without water and winced as the pills struggled to go down my dry throat. I picked up my phone and found myself pressing Xavier's name. The phone didn't even ring twice before he picked up.

"Hello? Fallon? Hello? Can you hear me?"

"Yes, I can hear you. How are you doing Xavier?"

"Man…I'm better now that I've heard from you. I've been worried sick about you. Your phone has been going straight to voicemail."

"I know, I know. A lot has happened since the last time we spoke. I have so much to update you on. Will you be free for dinner later on? I can talk more in depth then."

"Wait, what? You're in Houston? What are you doing back here?"

"Xavier, I will tell you all about it tonight. Figure out a place for us to go. I'll meet you wherever."

"Okay I will. There's this Italian place that I always go to downtown that I think you'll like. I'll text you the address in a few. Is Taylor here with you?"

The sound of Taylor's name took me aback and I was silent for a few seconds.

"Fallon? Are you still there?"

"Yes I'm still here. No, Taylor isn't down here. All I'll say right now is that I may be moving back to Houston a little sooner than I'd planned. Don't forget to text me that address. I'll see you later Xavier." I rushed to hang up the phone before Xavier could ask any more questions. My medicine was kicking in and the pain in my chest subsided enough for me to get up and start my day.

I walked downstairs and could immediately smell biscuits baking. I walked into the kitchen and was hit with a moment of déjà vu; Chef Warren was at the stove flipping bacon, Bentley and Tone were sitting on the barstools behind the island joking and laughing, Draya was looking at her phone while sipping a mimosa and Goldie was at the head of the table reading the newspaper. Chef Warren turned around and seen me standing in the doorway.

"Good morning Fallon! Come on in and fix you a plate."

I smiled at him but instead of walking over towards the counter to fix my food, I made my way over to Goldie. Goldie saw me coming his way and put the paper down to acknowledge me.

"What's up Fallon? Are you going to get yourself something to eat?"

I paused for a second before extending my hand to Goldie.

"I thought about your offer, Goldie. We've got a deal."

About the Author

Danielle Davenport is a self-proclaimed 'Midwestern Belle' from Indianapolis, Indiana. Obsessed with books since she could form complete sentences, Danielle began writing in elementary school and won numerous awards for her short stories and poetry. She launched her first blog, aptly named Behind Her Bangs while still a student at the illustrious Alabama Agricultural and Mechanical University. After years of sharing short stories, poetry, and witty outtakes on current events in the news and pop culture on the now-defunct site, Danielle decided to take on her biggest challenge yet: writing a book. Faux is her first novel.

When she's not behind her computer writing or scrolling through her Twitter timeline, she can be found in Indianapolis debating basketball trivia with her son, Drew.

Want more of Danielle? Follow her on social media!
Twitter: @thedeenicole
Instagram: @thedeenicole
Facebook: Danielle Davenport
www.bydanielledavenport.com